THE POWER

CALL OF THE GODS

H.P. WARRINGTON

authorHOUSE®

AuthorHouse™
1663 Liberty Drive
Bloomington, IN 47403
www.authorhouse.com
Phone: 833-262-8899

Published by AuthorHouse 01/22/2021

ISBN: 978-1-6655-1479-8 (sc)
ISBN: 978-1-6655-1478-1 (hc)
ISBN: 978-1-6655-1480-4 (e)

Print information available on the last page.

Any people depicted in stock imagery provided by Getty Images are models,
and such images are being used for illustrative purposes only.
Certain stock imagery © Getty Images.

This book is printed on acid-free paper.

Because of the dynamic nature of the Internet, any web addresses or
links contained in this book may have changed since publication and
may no longer be valid. The views expressed in this work are solely those
of the author and do not necessarily reflect the views of the publisher,
and the publisher hereby disclaims any responsibility for them.

This book is dedicated to everyone who has supported me along the way. Thank you for encouraging me to make my dreams come true!

A special shout-out to Madisyn, Maximo, and Derek for inspiring the main characters.

PROLOGUE

There are some things a lot of people will never understand.
First, the strength it takes to find a way to start over. Second,
some things that may not seem real...are very, *very* real. The
human brain doesn't always process things the way they truly
are. Now, my story goes way back to the day I found out about
the Power. I was maybe about eight years old when that fateful
spring day came.

I can remember the heat. The somehow bittersweet heat sank
into the depths of my heart. I would never feel the same kind of
warmth again. The sun was in the center of the sky at high noon
on a Tuesday. This was the heat that would make you *want* to
walk outside. After the incredibly chilling winter, there was a
longing to be in the beating sun on the first day of spring.

A slight breeze rustled the leaves around me as I walked
down my secret path. It was a small dirt trail behind my house
where the grass stopped growing because I stomped it down
every time I walked on it. I guess it couldn't have been *that* much
of a secret, considering my mother watched me walk back there
almost every day.

There was something about the tall trees and the full
raspberry bushes lining my trail that always made me spend
hours back there admiring it. The very end of my special trail was
my favorite. At the end, after about a mile of walking, was a vast
clearing.

There was a soft hill a few yards after the forest cleared. At
the bottom of that hill was the most beautiful sight I can ever
recall seeing.

The meadow that stretched for miles after that hill was something words can barely describe. For as far as I could see, flowers were blooming everywhere. This place was magical. The flowers ranged from the softest of pinks to the deepest of violets. It smelled like heaven in this untouched stretch of land. It was a small patch untouched by human contamination.

There are two types of people in this world – ones who try to preserve the lands and ones who contaminate them. Whichever one you are decides what kind of person you will be in life. Your relationship with the land around you is quite like your human relationships. Will you have mutualistic relationships where both parties flourish because of each other, or will you be parasitic and drain those around you?

My times in this field were always extraordinary, especially on this day. Today was strange. There was a cool breeze drifting through the air. I never thought it was possible to sweat while having goosebumps at the same time.

I liked to sit in my little meadow and take in the wind. I would sit there for hours touching the petals of the flowers and counting the leaves on the stems. By the time I noticed a change, the sun drifted. It was now around four o'clock.

As I decided to finally stand, there was a sound like the cracking of ice behind me. I frowned, turning around slowly.

Had I not seen it with my own two eyes, I would have never believed it. A man stood there, his body slowly appearing as more ice fell. I was in awe! As the ice chipped off, I began to see him more clearly.

He was dressed in all black, a cloak covering the majority of his body and more than half of his face. His eyes were glowing beneath the cloak. I should have been terrified. I thought I was dreaming. This, however, was clearly not the case.

"Do not fear, young one," his voice carried across the field effortlessly. "I am not here to hurt you." The ground beneath his feet began to freeze over. Rather than let fear consume me, I felt anger. This man was destroying my beautiful field!

"You know, you shouldn't just freeze the flowers like that." I pointed out. "You're ruining my field."

"Nonsense, child." He dismissed me. "You must heed my warning."

I put my hands on my hips and gave him a dirty look, "What warning do you mean?"

"In ten short years, to this very minute, you will be given the power. This power is not a toy and is not to be taken lightly." He removed his hood, his eyes a dazzling blue with the darkest of hair atop his head.

"Power?" I asked.

"It is not a joke, young one. It is a dangerous, foul thing. You may come into these powers but you must not tell anyone. Everyone will believe you are evil." His voice was smooth, like the music you wanted to listen to on repeat. I didn't know if the chills I had were from his voice or the thirty-degree temperature drop around me.

He never broke eye contact with me. There was a constant chill practically stuck on my spine that would not go away.

"Alliana, I have warned you." His legs began to crumble into ice shards below him, traveling up his body. "They *will* kill you."

CHAPTER ONE

Certain things happen for a reason, I think everyone can agree on that. There is no real way to tell exactly what reason, but there most definitely is one.

I didn't have a clue how, but ten years in the future, I remembered I needed to go to that exact spot. I kept that with me until this very momentous day. The sun was about to reach its spot in the center of the sky as I made my way down the wooded path. The trees had grown old, some of them falling in the way of the trail I hadn't gone down in over five years.

Uncertain of how, I outgrew my special field. At some point, it no longer appealed to me to sit in the sea of flowers and breathe in the serenity around me. An unknown excitement overtook me at the idea of seeing that man again. I hadn't learned his name, but I could describe in vivid detail what he looked like, and how his body shattered into ice as he disappeared.

He was an anomaly. I had never seen him before that day, nor had I seen him anywhere else in my life. A part of me truly believed that I dreamed the whole thing. There was no ice man waiting for me to come into my mystical powers. There was something so...new about this idea. It was an exciting overturn of my seemingly boring and dull life.

Living in a small town was just as draining as living in the city. There was no way to find peace unless you made it for yourself. That is the same for any place at any time. I felt myself becoming miserable as of late. I knew the only true way for me to get out of it would be to force myself out of it.

So, with that decision in mind, I made the second decision to risk everything and find this ice man again.

Arriving at the field for the first time in five years was overwhelmingly disappointing. The wonders that I once felt there as a child were gone. The weather drastically changed. This time of year, ten years ago, it was almost summer, and now it was barely 50 degrees. My sweater was not enough to shield me from the high winds stringing through the valley. The vast majority of the flowers that once comforted me were wilted, dying in the cold weather approaching.

I sat on the ground, looking up to the sky. The sun left a nice, warm coat on my skin as the goosebumps settled. There was something about this field that brought me to my inner peace. I didn't feel rushed or looked down upon. I felt normal. I felt so inconceivably normal that I never wanted to leave.

After a while of sitting there, I realized what I was doing. I was just…sitting. I was waiting for someone who, for the record, could have *totally* been my eight-year-old imagination. I chuckled aloud, realizing how much of a fool I made of myself. This man – the *ice man* – was never real in the first place. I kept that dream with me all of these years for it to be just that – a dream. He said that I would develop this *power*, one that I never even came close to experiencing.

I stood and looked down to brush myself off.

The air around me felt as if it suddenly dropped in degree. I froze, still looking down at my legs as I brushed them off. I could feel the color draining from my face as I slowly lifted my head.

I breathed a sigh of relief when I saw nothing standing in front of me. I must've been numb to the cold until I regained my focus.

"Welcome back, Alliana." His voice was smooth – just like I remembered. If a voice could be cold, that would be his. I whipped my body around towards the sound. My jaw dropped as I saw him again for the first time in ten years.

"Y-you…I –" I stuttered over my words, finally realizing that my imagination did not get the best of me all those years ago. He

2

was dressed in all white. It was a contrast from the first time I saw him, but certainly more fitting of his chilling character. His bright, crystal blue eyes sparkled in the sunlight around us. He had not aged at all since the last time I'd seen him.

"I figured you would be wanting to see me." He replied. "I know these things can be a bit...rough."

I stood there, in an unnecessary silence. I had no idea what to say to him. What *could* I say to him? He was clearly a being of another world. There was no way I could have a casual conversation with him.

"Sorry about the chill, I cannot really help that. It just rolls right off of me." The wind rustled his otherwise perfectly styled hair.

"You're real..." I muttered in disbelief. I put my hand over my mouth in an attempt to gather my thoughts.

"As shocking as that may be, we need to begin our work now. I can tell your Power is with you." He began. "There is no real way to tell when it will come out...but this is not the place to find out. Not in this world."

"This world? What other world even is there?" I scoffed in disbelief.

"Come," he reached his hand out to me, "I can show you things you have never even dreamed of."

At this point, him being real was enough to convince me something was happening. I reached out slowly. Our fingertips barely brushed and I felt a jolt of the coldest air I had ever felt in my life. I gasped loudly, attempting to jerk my hand back. He grabbed my wrist with his other hand, pulling me into him as the scenery around us faded.

Suddenly, I landed hard on stone. My legs gave out beneath me and I fell to the ground. The heat quickly wrapped around me. I was still shivering from the absolute cold he put me through. I looked down at my hands. They turned purple from those few short moments I touched his fingertips.

He stood on the other side of the room, unphased. He looked at me, waiting for me to get a grip on myself. I stood up, allowing the heat around me to seep into my skin. I looked around. The drastic difference in lighting took me off guard. It looked like the inside of a castle. The walls were a dark brick-looking material and torches were the only lighting system.

"You will get used to it." He said, beckoning for me to follow him. "There are many things you need to learn before we continue."

I quickly followed behind him in the hallway. I took in my surroundings as I walked. There were so many things going on all at once, I could barely concentrate on following the man in front of me. At that point, I realized I didn't even know his name. I stopped walking even as he continued on.

"Hey," I said quietly, with no response. "*Hey!*"

He stopped, turning around with his eyebrows furrowed. "What is it?"

"Can we take a second? Please?" I scoffed. "I've known you for two minutes and now I'm in some castle. I don't even know your name!"

"I don't have a name." He replied coldly. "I am the God of Frost. You may call me that."

"That's...a mouthful. I'll call you Frost." I offered.

"Do you think that it is respectful to call me that when I am thousands of years older than you?"

"Do you think I'm going to sit here and grovel at your feet?" I snapped back. "You've snatched the wrong girl then. You can send me home now if that's what you were looking for, *Frost.*"

The ground beneath us began to tremble and dust fell from the ceiling. As soon as I noticed, it stopped. I looked up at Frost, who smirked at me.

"It is here." He nodded.

"*What's* here?"

"The Power. It is with you." Without another word, he turned and continued down the hallway.

I sighed, before ultimately deciding to follow him. I hadn't realized how long the hallway was until I looked back and couldn't see the other room we started in. It was surprisingly warm in the hallway.

We arrived at a set of double doors. Frost stopped and turned to me once more. When he looked at me, the bright sparkle in his eye dimmed into a faint flame from a nearby torch.

"When you walk into this room, you will be overwhelmed. There are many Powers stored here. This is where most of the training will happen. You can ask any question you would like once we go in." He took a deep breath and swung the doors open. The surge of energy coming from that room was indeed overwhelming.

The room resembled that of a colosseum. Pillars superficially held up the ceiling and there were rows of stands on the edges of the room. On the back wall, there was a series of portraits. I only recognized one person out of the eight. Frost was in the middle, his strong gaze efficiently portrayed on the canvas.

"There are eight of us." He began. "We are older than time itself, it seems. You obviously know who I am. I am the God of Frost. The other powers are Water, Wind, Earth, Fire, Light, Healing, and Darkness. We, as a whole, create life as you know it. That field you were in every day, that was not an accident. We placed it there. You chose to keep it to yourself."

"Can I...can I look at the portraits?" I asked.

"You can touch them if you would like. For each one you touch, we will teach you that Power. Typically, you will only attach to one power, which is usually that of your mentor. We do not live in this realm, nobody lives in this realm. We only visit here. Each portrait you touch will take you another one. The specific realm of each God, that is." He explained, walking slowly towards the portraits. There was something about these pictures. They seemed too vivid in detail.

We started on the left. The first portrait was of a tall, strong-looking man. He had dark brown hair and emerald green eyes. He had a strong jawline and what looked like a scar across his right cheek.

"Now, before you do this, you should know something." Frost

watched my every move as I turned to look at him. His eyes met mine with a cold intensity.

"What is it?"

"Each of these is a challenge. The challenges prove you worthy. I cannot rescue you from these. I will be there, but I cannot protect you from whatever comes for you. At the end, you will be met with me and the God or Goddess who the challenge belongs to. Difficulty depends on the specific God." His eyes flashed with some...worry, maybe? "Choose wisely."

"What happens if...if I fail?"

"You die."

"Well, isn't that bright and dandy." I scoffed, rolling my eyes. "What if I choose not to do them?"

"I guess you could go home, but the people around you will find out about your Power eventually. There is no hiding something as strong as that. So, yes, you can go back without learning to control it, but life will never be the same for you again." He explained. "Without learning how to control it, you are a danger to everyone around you."

"So, I can die, or I can go home and die?" I frowned, crossing my arms over my chest.

"I do not make the rules, Alliana. I am just trying to help you." He replied, his posture still perfect.

"And why would you want to help me?" I tilted my head a bit to the side, raising my eyebrow.

"Because I am your mentor. Somebody will take the fall for your death and it will not be you." He said coldly, gesturing to the portraits. "Pick one to start with. We will be waiting for you at the end."

After being thrown into this, believing in Frost's existence for so long, I didn't think there was anything that could stop me from becoming what I was meant to be.

I thought about that for a second. "Becoming what I was meant to be" sounds so vague and ridiculous. Is there anything I am truly meant to be? I had no true purpose and no idea what I even wanted to do with my life either.

It was this...or a disappointed, widowed mother, and a sympathetic best friend who would never truly understand my situation. I had nothing to go back to. I took a deep breath and really considered if I wanted to risk my life like this.

Then I realized...people risk their lives every day. People risk their lives going to work or to school every day. If I could do something better for myself, why was I still just standing there?

I gave Frost one long, determined look. A somewhat prideful smile drifted onto his face as he watched me come to my decision. He gave me a small nod.

"I've never believed in someone as I believe in you, Alliana." He swallowed thickly, watching as the gears turned in my head.

"If I make it to you at the end, Frost," I returned a smile, "call me Alli."

I turned towards the portrait of the man and reached forward to it without hesitation. As soon as my fingertips touched the canvas, I felt my body being ripped through it into blackness.

CHAPTER TWO

With a decent thump, I landed on the soft, grassy land. While I caught my breath, I looked around to take in my surroundings. Despite my heart racing, everything seemed so natural. The area around me was much brighter than the dimly lit colosseum I was just in.

This place seemed like...serenity. It was beautiful. Everything was peaceful and nothing was out of place. There was a bright sun in the middle of the sky, and as I looked around, I saw a vaguely familiar field. Flowers stood strong in the heat that would usually wilt them. This was *my* field, the field I had grown so fond of as a child.

"Listen closely, for you only have one chance." A gravelly voice echoed throughout the sky. "Every move could be your last, look to the ground to see your past. There, you will learn the secrets in one glance."

Just as quickly as the voice was echoing, it was gone. I took a deep breath. I took one step forward. The ground shook with tremendous energy. If I had not moved back when I did, I would have fallen into a bottomless hole. I gasped, but as quickly as the ground fell away beneath me, it reappeared just moments later.

Taking one more deep breath, I spun around to look towards a familiar onset of woods. I tested the ground in front of me with my foot. There was no rumbling from deep within the Earth. I put my weight down.

I felt myself fall as I lifted my other foot. I gripped onto the edge of the ground where it broke off under me. I cried out as the rest of my body dangled. I could feel the dirt gathering in my fingernails as I held on.

Let go, Alliana! A voice drifted through my head. *Let go or you will never make it out of there! Do it now!*

Frost. The voice belonged to Frost.

"I can't!" My arms began to shake from holding my weight. The dirt was causing my hands to slip.

If you do not let go, you will be buried alive! Let go now!

Fear coursed through me. Chills ran up my spine as I realized the hole was slowly being covered again. I had no choice other than to trust him. With less than a second before the hole was covered, I let go.

A scream ripped from my throat as I plummeted. It seemed endless. The wind rushed past my ears as the endless fall continued. I reached out to find something, anything, but could not reach it.

I closed my eyes to brace myself for impact. I was standing now, too scared to open my eyes. My racing heart slowed as I realized I was okay. I slowly opened my eyes, sighing in relief.

I was back in my field at the exact spot that I fell from. Before I even realized what I was doing, I sat on the ground below me. I tried to remember what the gravelly voice said when I first arrived. Something about my past, secrets, and making choices. Wasn't this supposed to be the *Earth* challenge? Why did my past matter in the Earth challenge?

After regaining my composure, I stood again. I brushed myself off with a sigh. I looked over at the field, taking a deep breath. I saw a child out running in the field and laughing as she played all by herself.

I walked forward without thinking and was rewarded with the ground staying intact below me. I stopped where the flowers began, watching the little girl in the field. She had an aura around her, a bright, blue color that engulfed the area she was in.

A figure appeared on the far side of the field. I quickly recognized it as Frost. I frowned, realizing the situation before me.

She had long, sandy brown hair that flowed gently behind her in the wind. She had eyes that matched her hair almost exactly. A realization hit me suddenly - that little girl playing in the field was *me*. The aura around her was also around me. I seemed much younger than eight in the field, maybe I was five or six. I met Frost at eight years old. What was Frost doing around me at this time? Was this a memory?

It couldn't be a memory. I was seeing myself. This was a story...but whose story was it? Frost looked over at me from his position in the field. Even from as far away as he was, I could see the look in his eyes.

There were stories beyond my years. There were stories he shared with me I knew nothing about. I didn't know who Frost was before I turned eight, but he knew exactly who I was. How long had he followed me? How long had he watched over me before I finally knew of his existence?

I walked forward, my eyes never leaving his. Eventually, I made it over to the younger version of myself. Although she could not see Frost, she stopped as I approached her. She watched me with her head tilted to the side. How could she see me, but not Frost?

"Who are you?" She – I? - asked gently. "This is my field. You can't be here."

"You'll know soon enough..." I whispered to her. "Nothing lasts forever." I gazed around at the beautiful field that only begun to wilt as time went on. Nothing would last forever, and nothing would stay the same.

"You can't be here." She repeated. "Go."

"You can trust me, Alliana." I told her. "I won't tell anyone about your field." I smiled at her, watching, as her eyebrows furrowed.

"You're stepping on my flowers, you know." She put her hands on her hips. "If you're gonna be here, you gotta get off my flowers." She was naïve. I could see it within myself.

I nodded, stepping off of the flowers.

I looked back to where Frost was standing. He disappeared.

There was something about this area that was so calming. I never understood why I kept coming to this field. As I grew older, the values I had when I was younger didn't seem to follow me.

And I stood there, watching that field from a whole new perspective. I watched as my younger self grew taller and older. The field had always been strong and vibrant when I was there every day. Maybe the magic in the field wasn't so...natural after all. Maybe magic *was* real and only existed in certain places.

This field was the closest to magic I ever came to in my younger years. I watched, from that same spot I was standing, as Frost introduced himself to me for the first time. The blue aura, that had once been so vibrant and strong around me, dissipated. It was still noticeable, but it was fading.

And then I watched, for what felt like seconds, as the sun rose and set hundreds of times. I still came to the field every day until I was twelve years old. I watched as I came every other day, every two days, to just once a week.

Soon enough it became never. I was thirteen when I stopped coming to the field altogether. As the time-lapse continued, the flowers began to wilt. Without my presence, the area grew colder and the field became...sad.

There was something so overwhelming about the sight in front of me I wasn't sure how to react. Tears welled in my eyes as I watched what was once my favorite place – my safe place – fade into nothing in front of me. I left my field to die, and with it, my younger self as well.

Finally, I watched my present-self stumble into the field from the trail that was now overgrown. My once long hair was now neatly cut at my shoulders. My once soft and loving brown eyes were now hard and cold. The aura around me faded so much so that all that was left was a thin line of it.

The magic faded from me. It almost gave up on me. I always wondered why my field died so quickly. It was simple. The magic from the field was actually magic from me.

A single tear rolled down my cheek as I heard two pairs of footsteps behind me. I quickly wiped it away as I turned around to face Frost and the same man from the portrait. He was much taller than Frost. His eyes reflected a bright green as the sun hit them.

They stopped a few feet in front of me. There was an approving look in Frost's eyes. I looked towards the other man – assumingly the God of Earth – and prepared to hear what he had to say.

"You are wondering what this has to do with Earth, aren't you?" He asked. I recognized his gravelly voice from earlier. He was the one who told me the riddle.

"A little, yes." I nodded.

"The Earth around you needs nourishing, always." He began. "People take the Earth for granted all the time. The beautiful greens, blues, pinks, and yellows of nature cannot flourish on their own. It is the same with human emotion."

He looked at Frost, his face softening. I met Frost's gaze. A chill ran up my spine in the process.

"Your take on life, your views, were what caused this meadow to grow. We, of course, planted the seeds, but you nourished them. At least until you stopped coming. The field fed your Power. As soon as you stopped coming, it was evident in you and in the field that there was nearly nothing left." Within Frost's voice, there was a message. I couldn't quite figure out what it was.

"I think I understand." I nodded.

"Some things need constant flourishing, Alliana." Frost replied. "Come with me. I will take you back to the portraits."

He reached his hand out to grab mine. Expecting the icy chill this time, I grabbed his hand quickly, and everything spun around us. He pulled me closer to him again, his hand wrapping around my wrist.

Towards the end this time, I saw the frame of the portrait. On the canvas was the colosseum. We shot through it at an incredible speed, leaving me to crumble on the ground again as Frost stood on the other side of the room. I rolled to a stop against a pillar, grunting as I smacked into it.

"What happened to that getting easier?" I groaned, lying on my back.

"It will take a while until you have control over your Power." He said. "Did you learn anything from this challenge?"

"Well," I climbed to my feet, "I learned that someone helped me."

"What do you mean?" He questioned, his eyebrows wrinkling.

"When I fell you talked to me." I pushed. "You said you weren't allowed to do that."

He looked around the room cautiously. He sighed, realizing there was no one else in the room.

"I am not supposed to." He replied, crossing his arms. "You must not tell anyone of that, Alliana."

"Is it really that big of a deal?" I frowned.

"More than you are allowed to know at the moment." He replied gravely. "But come, you must try to use your new power."

"What am I supposed to do?" I asked.

"It is your power. I do not know how to make it happen. You chose Earth first, that Power has been embedded within you. Try it. Concentrate." His voice was soothing. I closed my eyes, breathing slowly. I lifted my hand, something I never felt before coursed through me.

I opened my eyes, and suddenly, everything around me was green. I gestured towards one of the pillars and watched as hundreds of tiny flowers sprouted from it. Terrified, I pulled my hand back and held it to my chest.

The world around me faded back to the dim, torchlit area I saw previously. The pillar was still covered in flowers as I walked towards it.

"All it takes, Alliana, is concentration. Soon enough, it will be second nature. With Earth, you must be careful. At times, the God of Earth has gotten too angry, and you have seen the result. Earthquakes are made that you blame on your tectonic plates. How would the plates move without a significant force? This is the role he plays."

14

He waved his hand. The flowers on the pillar wilted quickly and died, falling on to the floor below.

"But come, you must finish the challenges."

There were six left. This was going to be a long day.

"Oh, before you pick," Frost interjected, "pay close attention to the riddles they give you in the beginning. Those will save your life."

"You mean if you don't save me first?" I raised my eyebrows at him. The hard look on his face shut my question down quickly. I nodded slowly, turning back to the portraits.

The portrait next to the God of Earth's was one of a dainty woman. She had long, blonde hair that drifted below her waist. Her eyes sparkled a bright, blue color. She was dressed in all white, similar to Frost.

I picked her next. She couldn't be that bad.

And boy, was I wrong.

CHAPTER THREE

T he ground below me was soft. After looking around for a brief moment, I found another place I recognized easily. I was standing in the middle of my village, except I was presented with a ghost town. I turned to look behind me, seeing the dainty woman from the portrait.

Her eyes looked brighter than they were in the portrait. She crossed her arms over her chest with her head held high. She closed her eyes, lifting her head up to the sky.

The wind around us picked up to an insane speed. Her hair whipped around her, but the rest of her body was still. She was, otherwise, unaffected by the strong winds.

Listen closely, for you shall hear, within the souls of those who died, buried far but near, all of your answers lie inside.

"Great," I muttered under my breath, "that was really frickin' helpful."

As she faded into the gusts of wind, they became stronger. The leaves that fell on the ground during the long fall were swirling in circles in the air. I gulped. There was only one reason the leaves would be doing that, only one reason this time would relate to me.

I turned back around, seeing the tornado slowly starting to form behind me. It whipped around willfully, almost as if it knew exactly what it was doing.

I backed up slowly, stumbling over my own feet as I fell down. Despite the chill in the atmosphere, my body was drenched in sweat. My hands shook as they never had before. I could barely get to my feet before the tornado began racing towards me. I turned my back to it ran, trapped in what seemed like an endless run of my village. It was familiar but strange. Everything seemed different.

There was only one other time that I saw a tornado.

I was about seven years old when it happened. That pivotal day left my mother a widow and me without a father.

I ran towards the door of one of the houses, attempting to open it. The door would not open no matter how hard I tugged it. I cursed under my breath. I could feel the tornado pulling me backward. I knew I had to fight it. There was nothing that could stop me.

Well...except for maybe a giant tornado.

I remembered we had a community shelter. It was too hard for the architects to craft basements for every house, so they made one for the whole community.

We were a small town, so the fortitude of it held everyone. I took a shaky breath, quickly attempting to remember where the shelter was.

I closed my eyes and, just for a second, the wind was gone. I heard laughter and happy voices roaming around the village. I smiled to myself, remembering the days where everyone was happy.

The shelter was in the center of the town, beneath the house of the founder. As soon as I opened my eyes, the wind started slamming the doors and shattering windows. Now, it was time for my deepest fear to be relived. I started running. At this point, I didn't even know where I was running to.

The village was not exactly the same as it had always been. There were more houses. They kept repeating over and over again. I finally reached the founder's home. Nobody had lived there in decades, but it still stood in the center of the town.

I reached for the door and a strong force pulled me back towards the tornado. I gasped as the breath rushed out of my lungs. My body was thrown into the brick of the founder's home. The glass of the window next to me shattered.

I coughed, unable to lift myself up off the wall. I suddenly fell to the ground. My legs crumpled under me and forced me onto the cement below. The tornado neared closer and closer. I couldn't move from my spot no matter how much I willed myself to move.

"Alliana!" A voice ripped through the air. There was a figure running from the side of the building. As he got closer, I began to realize who he was.

The same man I inherited my hair, eyes, nose, and smile from was running after me.

"Alliana!" He called.

"Daddy!" A small, whiny voice I recognized as my own called out to him. I looked down at myself again and realized that I had taken on the form of my younger self. I reached out to my father as he got closer to me.

He picked me up with ease, throwing me over his shoulder in the process. He pulled the door open and ran into the building. The shelter resided in the back end of the home. He quickly ran towards it.

"It's okay, Alli, I've got you." He whispered. His fingers ran soothingly through my hair. Tears flooded my eyes as I remembered this critical day. My life would never be the same after this.

I screamed as the roof was torn from the building. The far side of it was ripped from the ground and flew into the sky. I could feel my father using every last bit of his strength to get me away from the raging storm behind us.

Once we made it to the edge of the building where the shelter was, I saw my mother waiting at the top of the steps.

"Alli!" She called, reaching her arms out for me. I would never have realized I was crying if I didn't touch my face. My cheeks were soaked and now caked with mud.

With one last shout, my dad practically threw me into my mother's arms. I only had two seconds to look back in time to see my father's body sucked into the tornado. A scream escaped his lips.

"Daddy!" I shouted. I turned around and saw that I separated from my younger self. I didn't have more than three seconds to think – should I run or should I go into the shelter? Would the shelter protect me or would the woods protect me?

Listen closely, for you shall hear, within the souls of those who died, buried far but near, all of your answers lie inside.

With one of my three seconds left, I hoped I understood what that meant. My *father* was the one who died. He was buried far, but near, and all of my answers would lie inside. Inside of *what*?

"Oh, you've got to be kidding me." I muttered, before realizing I had no other choice (or at least, no time to think of another choice). I heard the shelter doors close and bolt behind me.

There was only one option. With one last boost of personal confidence, I took a running start at the tornado in front of me. Before I could take more the three steps, the storm pulled me from the ground and into the wind.

I screamed. There was nothing else I could do. I swirled around with all of the random debris in the tornado. Things were moving so quickly. I couldn't even gather a logical thought.

And before I knew it, everything went black.

Not even two seconds later, I was standing in a perfectly calm, cloud-like city. There was a slight, steady breeze that blew my hair off my shoulders. I took a deep breath, feeling my racing heart start to calm.

There were few words to describe the place I was standing before. It was a castle surrounded by clouds. The brick was pure white, almost too bright to look at. The pillars stood tall and the gate rolled open as I approached.

I didn't know exactly where I was. Was this where you go after you die? Was I *dead*? Did I make the wrong choice?

I proceeded forward carefully. Anxiety crept onto me as I walked into the doors of the palace. I was greeted with two familiar faces – Frost and the Goddess of Wind.

The room was vast in front of me. The walls were a pure, white color. The flooring was made of crystals. You could see through the bottom of it. There were clouds and different birds passing by at incredibly fast speeds.

I took in the area around me. It required a deep

understanding. We were up in the sky, so far that nobody with normal vision would be able to see it. There was something so... spectacular about it.

There were large birds on perches all along the walls. There was a gentle swish of wind that trailed through the palace, despite it being closed off completely from the outside.

"You understood the riddle." She almost sounded disappointed. "Unfortunately, sometimes life makes you relive your worst moments. You must face all of your fears to overcome the new fears you will obtain."

"Fears are endless." Frost continued for her. "You must become accustomed to overcoming your fears because you will only gain more as you get older. Once you start carrying on with your life, different phases bring about different fears."

"I understand." I nodded.

"You are strong, Alliana." Frost told me, nodding. "You completed the past two challenges with intelligence, something I look for in my trainees."

The Goddess of Wind glanced at him, taking his gaze away from mine. I couldn't see what was exchanged between the two of them, but it made Frost clear his throat.

"The loss of your father will be carried with you, but you have faced your fear. You are no longer *afraid* of what happened to your father. You can embrace it now. That is something you will take with you for the rest of your life." He nodded, walking towards me. "Follow me. I will take you back to the other portraits."

I nodded, following him as he turned. The Goddess of Wind stared at me as I walked behind him. There was something in her eyes, some sort of *intent*, that I could not quite put my finger on. Something told me she was going to be an enemy.

"Do not worry about her, Alliana." Frost mentioned as we walked through the palace. It was much like the dark halls he had taken me through to get to the portraits before, but naturally lighter. There were so many questions I had, but I couldn't quite get any out.

"What do you mean?" I asked. Well, I guess *that* was a question, just not one I was thinking of.

"She is a bit...stand-offish. You will get used to her eventually. She does not have a problem with you if that was what you were thinking." He stopped in the middle of the hallway, sighing. "But you do have to be careful. Not all of the Gods will have your best interest in mind. Some would benefit more if you died and did not understand their riddles."

"Is that supposed to make me feel better?" I replied, furrowing my eyebrows.

"No, of course not. But you need to be careful of who you trust." He looked at me as if he was worried. I saw that look a lot with him. He seemed to be constantly worried. I didn't know if that was about me personally, or if my completing all of the challenges mattered more than I thought.

"How do I know I can trust you?" I asked him.

"Well..." He turned and kept walking. "You do not know that. You will never know that until I can prove it to you, that is if I get the opportunity to prove it to you."

I stood there for a moment before following him.

"Oh, and by the way," he turned towards me, "you may want to brush your hair before continuing on with the trials." I saw the smallest hint of a smile and I opened my mouth to say something, anything really, and nothing would come out.

We reached the end of the hallway and saw the familiar frame. I was almost comforted by the dark, firelit walls of the colosseum. This was how it was going to be for me from now on. Not much changed. It was always me against the world. Now, it was me against...well, all of the worlds.

I reached through the canvas, feeling myself getting pulled through it once again. This landing was a bit smoother than the last few. I landed hard on my feet but still managed to stay on them.

"You are learning how to handle it, Alliana." Frost nodded, keeping his perfect posture. "You learn quickly. That is good."

"Didn't I tell you to call me Alli?" I asked him, tilting my head to the side.

"That is incredibly informal. I do not like informalities."

"Well, Frost," I chuckled, "you're just going to have to get used to that."

CHAPTER FOUR

C old swept through my body. I felt like I was floating. I gasped, then took a deep breath. I was met with salt. The air around me was riddled with it. I tried to move and it felt like my arm was in slow motion. A splash came from beside me as I moved.

I opened my eyes. I was treading water in the open ocean. I spun around multiple times to try and see anything that would help me. Fear settled within me, my heart racing. I felt pressure on my spine. It was nothing other than the crushing anxiety of being stranded alone in the middle of the ocean.

My breath was shaky. I couldn't think, but I attempted to keep my head above water. There was a sinking feeling in my stomach. The feeling wouldn't shake as I tried to slow my breathing.

"Welcome to my realm, Alliana." His voice flowed like, well, *water*. It was like a river that slowly joined into the ocean.

"Yes, I feel very welcome." I sighed.

Underneath the heavy waves, the sea below will leave you dazed, you can make it in one breath, just to travel to the deepest depth.

I heard thunder in the distance and quick to follow was a bolt of lightning. Rain began pouring down, pelting onto my head harder than I thought was possible. The waves around me began to pick up.

I grimaced, quickly coming to the realization that a small ring of water around me was completely calm. I didn't realize how heavy I was breathing until I heard it bounce back towards me.

In the distance, a wave began to form. It was racing towards my location at an extraordinary speed, gaining considerable size on the way. Despite being in the water, I was sweating. The wave was almost to me. I closed my eyes and held my arm up to shield my face.

I braced myself for the strength of the wave to pull me under, but after a few seconds, there was nothing. I opened my eyes, now seeing waves smash into an invisible barrier around me. I exhaled in relief, but my relief was short-lived.

I felt something grab my foot and yank me down. I screamed, but it was cut off by water coursing into my lungs. I choked and looked down to see what grabbed me. Whatever it was, the fingernails were long and jagged. I tried to jerk my foot away. I watched as the surface of the water got farther and farther away.

The dizziness began to set in as I attempted to hold my breath. The borders of my vision began fading to black.

I saw a figure next to me. It followed me down to the bottom of the ocean. I recognized Frost's face as he reached out to me. Was I imagining this?

Concentrate, Alliana.

I saw a clear concern in his eyes.

Concentrate!

Without thinking, I took a deep breath. I reached out to him as I expected my body to convulse. I was surprised when I realized that I was breathing. Frost's image disappeared and I regained the little consciousness I had lost. I looked down, seeing a tail rushing us down towards the bottom of the ocean.

Her hair flowed behind her, looking perfectly dry despite us being underwater. Whoever she was, she had *scales*. There was no way she was even *partially* human. There was a distant light we were following towards the bottom of the ocean.

She looked back at me and I almost screamed. Her face resembled a goblin. She had no eyes and wrinkly skin. There was a hole where her lips should be and pointy, jagged teeth lining it. I feared for my life in more ways than one now.

She yanked me down to be on her level, staring at me in spite of her absent eyes. Sea animals began to gather around us – sharks, a variety of fish, and even a squid.

"You will die down here." Her voice was hoarse like she didn't get to use it much.

"You're wrong." I said, standing my ground. "I am more powerful than you." The surge of confidence had come from nowhere, but considering she couldn't even see, I liked my odds.

"*I* belong here," she rasped, "*You* are an intruder."

The animals around us became restless. A shark swam past me and slammed into my side. I gulped. I was unsure of what to do with the now thousands of fish surrounding us.

"*They* know that," she cackled, "but do *you*?"

Another shark rammed into me as it opened its jaws to eat one of the fishes around us. Fear began to course through my veins. The pressure from being so deep in the ocean was making my head pound. It felt like the water was going to make my head cave in!

"You don't scare me." I said. "You are nothing but a minion in this realm. I could take it over." I lifted my hand. One of the sharks came to my side and circled me. It watched my every move.

Her face wrinkled even more as I raised my eyebrow at her.

"*They* know that, but do *you*?" I asked, gesturing towards her. The shark flew from my side, opened its mouth wide, and chomped down onto her flank. She screamed loudly as the shark dragged her in the opposite direction.

I breathed a sigh of ease as I watched all of the animals disperse. I gave myself a moment to calm down and began to swim towards the light. I had a new-found confidence in my Power at that point.

Frost was right. All it took was a bit of concentration.

Just as I calmed, the same creature grabbed me again. When I looked up, I saw the chunk taken out from the shark bite. She wasn't even bleeding.

"You will *never* take this realm, you will-!" Before she could even finish her sentence, another shark came and bit her head, severing it from her body. I screamed, nearly catapulting my body away from her.

27

I couldn't remember a time I ever swam faster than I did at that moment. I guess the shark was a formidable ally. I continued on towards the light, hoping this challenge ended once I got there.

The light was actually the beginning of a well-lit cave. I swam inside of it, taken aback in shock at what I saw.

Everyone says Atlantis is fake, but there was no other way to describe this place. There was a castle, just about a hundred of those weird mermaid ladies, and normal looking people just walking around.

Once I got to the path that led to the castle gates, I felt my feet touch solid ground. I was on my feet and walking. I had never been so grateful to walk in my life! I approached the gates. Despite being underwater, they still creaked as they slowly opened.

I walked in, taking in the coral reef lining the entirety of the cave walls. There were blue, green, purple, red, and pink corals. The palace reflected the colors exquisitely. I walked through the front door. The door itself had to be at least twenty feet high with double doors meeting at the top in a point.

The inside of the palace was a hard, marble looking floor. It was white with blue specks throughout. I walked across it. I was no longer in water and I was completely dry. I wasn't sure how the atmosphere in here worked, but I was thankful I wasn't soaked.

I walked down a hallway, running my fingers along the wall as I walked. It had a smooth feel to it. It was eerily calm within the palace. I took a deep breath and wondered where I should go next. The hallway split in three different directions. Frost and the God of Water had to be down one of these hallways.

The choice was mine to make, but I was of scared what else could be waiting on the other side of the two halls they weren't in. I closed my eyes and tilted my head to the ceiling. The chandelier swung slightly although the air was absolutely still.

I felt a pull like I needed to follow it. I looked to the right. My eyes suddenly widened I saw what looked like snow down the hallway. I looked down the middle hall and saw what resembled slime. The hallway to the left looked the same. I closed my eyes again and when I opened them, those things were gone.

I turned towards the right and followed down the chamber quickly. It suddenly spread out into a large room. Now, what was *in* that room stopped me in my tracks.

"You have *got* to be kidding me." I muttered under my breath.

Before me was the biggest crab I had ever or would ever see in my life. It had to be at least fifteen feet tall, and the width almost covered the entirety of the room. His pinchers were bigger than my entire body!

The challenge wasn't anywhere near over yet, I guessed.

As soon as I passed the threshold of the room, one of his pinchers raced down towards me. I quickly jumped back beyond the door. I watched as his claw snapped the solid, stone door in two. The half he broke off slammed onto the floor, shattering into giant pieces.

"Why me?" I groaned. I stood flat against the wall behind the fully intact door. "Of *course,* this happens to me."

I closed my eyes, reliving the whole challenge I had just faced. I recalled controlling the sharks. If I controlled the sharks, maybe I could control this crab. Hopefully, I could control him for long enough so I could get across without being snapped in two.

Wishful thinking, I assumed.

For starters, I had no idea how I controlled the sharks in the first place. Second, there was probably a lot more concentration involved in controlling an animal nearly fifty times your size.

I sighed and realized that it was either going to kill me trying, or I'd be stuck here forever.

Maybe living in this luxurious palace wouldn't be too bad after all.

The only way to do this was to face it head-on. Confidence and courage are a necessity in this sort of situation, I learned. Of course, I learned that the hard way, but I guess that's the best way.

I stepped away from my spot and passed the threshold once more. I lifted my hand, forcing the crab to look at me. Whatever I was trying to do was apparently not working. He lifted his claw again and got ready to snap me in half.

Mind control was out of the equation. I quickly lifted my head. I felt the wind speed up in the room. Wind was...not what I was going for, but it worked a little. I gestured towards the other half of the stone door. It ripped from its hinges and flew right into the crab's pincher before it could reach me.

Again, the door crumbled in his claw. I covered my head as I ran. The chunks of stone showered down on me. I was about halfway to the other side. A noise came from it that I never thought a crab could make. I lifted the stones and sent them flying at the crab to distract him as I ran towards the other side.

I looked back and saw his claw coming for me once again. With a loud grunt, I leaped, hoping I would make it. I landed with a hard thud on the other side, well in the hallway. I wheezed for breath, taking in how hard I had actually hit the marble floor.

The crab was trying to get his claw through the threshold, but every time he attempted to pass the border, sparks flew across the room. He bounced backward. I crawled towards the door at the far end and hoped that this challenge was over.

I panted heavily as I pushed myself to my feet. Even if this challenge wasn't over yet, I had to continue on no matter what.

As I carried on, I realized this had become less about me and more about Frost. For once, I had someone who *wanted* me to succeed, and I couldn't blow that. I couldn't disappoint the one person who expected the most of me. The proud look he got in his eyes when I completed these challenges was unlike anything I'd ever seen before.

I shook the thought from my mind, pushing the doors open. Standing before me, in the center of the room, was Frost and the God of Water.

There was a beaming smile on Frost's face. I didn't realize it right away, but that was the first time I'd ever seen him *actually* smile.

"Congratulations, Alliana. You have completed this challenge."

The God of Water nodded. "You completed this trial with confidence. That is not something we see often."

"Challenges vary from God to God as I mentioned before. The past two you chose had deep connections with you that you are unaware of. I worked endlessly with them to help you keep your Power." Frost explained. "And this challenge, although harder than most, was passed with flying colors."

CHAPTER FIVE

"T hat was excellent, Alliana." Frost told me once we arrived back in the colosseum. "Your confidence has improved quite a bit since we started." He straightened out his back and began walking away from the portraits.

"Where are you going?" I grimaced. "There are more challenges to do."

"Yes, Alliana, there are," He sighed. "but those will have to wait for another day. For now, you must rest to regain your strength. Come, I will show you to your room." He turned around once again and walked back down the long hallway.

The corridor seemed to stretch for an eternity as we walked around curves. We took a right I hadn't noticed on the way in and ended up at a staircase. We walked side by side up the stairs.

"Wait." He grabbed my arm, waiting to continue until I faced him. "There's something you need to know." There was a sparkle in his blue eyes from the torches lining the walls. I never realized how sharp, yet soft, his facial features were. He looked and felt as cold as ice.

Even those with the coldest hearts can be warm sometimes.

"These next few challenges...they will test your strength, Alli." He had a grim look on his face. "Promise me you'll be careful."

"Have I not been careful up until now?"

"I will not – I cannot help you in the next few challenges, not even mine. You need to be very, very careful. You must not tell anyone the ways I have helped." He looked down to where his hand was latched around my arm.

"What's bringing this about?" I asked as I followed his eyes. "You're acting weird."

"I-I guess I am...worried." He cleared his throat and removed his hand from my arm. "But, no matter, you must get some rest."

"Frost, wait –"

"I will *not* talk about it anymore." He shot me one more look that told me he meant business. "All I am worried about is losing my trainee before I need you. That is all."

I grumbled and waited for him to travel further up the stairs before I followed. He was acting strange. Frost never acted like this before. We stopped at the top of the stairs. There were eight rooms with four lined up on each side. The doors had to be at least twenty feet tall and reached to a point at the top.

He led me to the third door on the right. The middle of the door held an emblem. It was a dazzling blue color.

"Each God has an emblem," he explained quietly, "and they belong on our formal attire only. These are trainee quarters. Tomorrow, you will begin your physical training."

"Physical training?" I crinkled my nose.

"You, along with the other trainees, will...for lack of a better term, fight each other." He replied. "There is no other way to test your physical abilities. The others are already in bed. They have a step up on you."

He closed his eyes and put his hand on the emblem in the center of the door. A beam of light shot from it, lighting up the entire corridor. Once the light faded, the doors creaked open inward. The room within it was elegant.

The floor resembled snow. The chandelier was shaped like a snowflake. Smaller snowflakes dangling down released light from them. I looked around with my jaw dropped. The bed in the middle of the room was huge. The sheets were an immaculate, white color.

I walked forward and touched them. They were softer than anything I ever felt before in my life. I turned to look at Frost. His eyes glimmered and a small smile came upon his face as he watched me.

There was something so different about him today; there was something different about him in this light. For a moment, I forgot who he was, who I was, and even where we were. I wasn't sure what brought this along, but there was something unexplainable going on.

I felt a pain in my chest. It was a dull, barely-there pain, but a pain nonetheless.

"I need to go." He cleared his throat while looking at his feet. "You will find an ample amount of clothing in the closet to the right. If you need something, you must wait until the morning. However, everything you might need is in this room."

And that was true, *very* true until he walked out of the room.

The next morning was one of wonder. I woke up and walked into the closet he had mentioned. There was just about everything I could ever dream of. There were shoes, shirts, sweatshirts, pants, and shorts. There was literally anything I could ever want.

I found the bathroom as well. After freshening up for the day I picked an outfit. As I walked out of the bathroom, I heard a knock on the door. I frowned and walked over to open it. I pulled the doors open.

Frost stood there with his hair newly slicked back. He was wearing a pair of black pants and a white button-up shirt. He had the sleeves folded up to his arms and he was tying a tie around his collar as I met his eyes.

"Good morning, Alliana." He nodded at me. "You are due in the Hall in about ten minutes." He checked his watch with a raised eyebrow.

"Ten minutes?" I gasped. "Nice warning, Frost!" I groaned and ran towards the closet. I grabbed whatever I could find. I ended up with a pair of leggings and a white jacket with the same emblem from the door on it. I quickly tied my hair up with the hair tie on my wrist.

I looked over to see Frost watching me again. "Yes?" I asked.

35

"Nothing." He shook his head. "Nothing at all."

I grabbed a pair of tennis shoes and quickly put them on. Frost and I were dressed so differently, but the emblem embroidered on our sleeves were the same. I looked from mine to his before looking into his eyes.

"You are…wearing the appropriate attire for this event." He quickly turned and walked down the hall. I followed him with my arms crossed over my chest.

We passed a woman in a bright red dress. She had dark skin and even darker hair. She had the deepest brown eyes I'd ever seen. I was almost entranced by her. Since I never met her before, I was shocked by the smoothness of her voice.

"Good morning, God of Frost." She nodded towards him.

"To you, as well, Goddess of Fire." He bowed his head slightly before he continued to lead me past her. I didn't notice I wasn't breathing when she walked by until I took a deep breath once we passed her.

"Wow," I murmured. I shivered at the effect of her.

"She can be a lot to handle." Frost nudged my arm. "We should keep going."

At the bottom of the stairs, we took another right. We followed the hall down until it branched off into two. We took the left. We arrived at another set of doors and he pushed them open with ease. We were on a balcony, now staring down at the colosseum below us.

I walked to the edge of the balcony and saw seven other doors leading to more balconies. Different emblems were on each one.

I recognized the first few Gods I met – Wind, Water, and Earth – with their trainees on the balconies. I was in awe. For a while, I believed I was the only trainee. I now knew there were seven others.

"Alliana," Frost put his hand on my shoulder, "stand back. We are about to begin."

I made room for him next to me as he pulled us back away from the edge of the balcony. There was one balcony that had a lone trainee on it. The emblem on the front depicted a flame.

A burst of flame came from the middle of the colosseum floor. The Goddess of Fire appeared from the flame.

"Welcome, everyone!" She exclaimed as the fires by her feet went out slowly. "Today, we will introduce our trainees to the others. You have all completed half of the challenges. Today that means nothing. You will be tested in your *physical* prowess today. As trainees of Gods, you must prove your worth. You were chosen for a reason, and now, you will *prove* that reason."

I watched her in awe. She commanded the room with her presence. There was a charisma to her that was unmatched with anyone. Her red dress sparkled in the torchlit room. Her hair was full of kinky curls. It led down to the middle of her back.

"We will begin by introducing ourselves and our trainees. I would *love* to start." She gestured up towards her balcony. Another flame spouted from next to her, then faded away to reveal her trainee.

The only thing I could decipher from where I was is that he was blond. His hair was short and he had a no-nonsense type of look on his face. He would be a daunting opponent.

"This is Derek, trainee of me, the Goddess of Fire." She looked at him proudly. "*He* will, without a doubt, win this challenge. Now, Derek, show off your obtained skill."

His gaze met mine for a split second before his eyes turned a bright red. He lifted his hand and the flames upon all the torches roared up six or seven feet into the air. He put his hand down. His eyes faded back to their normal color. The torches slowly shrank back to normal. and he smirked.

With a large flame, both of them disappeared. They reappeared on their balcony. I looked from them to Frost.

"Do I have to do that?" I asked in a whisper. "I don't know how to use ice powers yet."

"Hush!" He snapped. "You do know. You just haven't channeled them yet. She knows that and she's doing this to embarrass me. You can do this Alliana, you just need to concentrate like in the Water challenge. I watched you the whole time. You know how to use concentration to better your Power."

The next two to appear with a quake of the earth was the God of Earth accompanied by his trainee. His trainee had a medium complexion with curly black hair atop his head. He had a suave look on his face. He knew exactly what he was there to do and he was going to do exactly that with no hesitation.

"This is Maximo." The God of Earth's voice rumbled throughout the colosseum. "He has the strength of a boulder and is ready for this challenge."

Maximo's eyes turned bright green, similar to the red in Derek's eyes. The ground began to shake beneath us until the whole colosseum was rumbling. A large crack formed in the ground around the God of Earth and Maximo.

Maximo's eyes faded back to their original color and they both appeared back on their balcony.

The Goddess of Light was next. I hadn't met her yet but she was beautiful. She had blonde hair so light it was almost pure white. Her eyes were yellow. Her trainee's name was Apolonia. She was a pretty girl with long black hair.

Next was the God of Healing. He had brown hair and was dressed in green. His eyes matched his shirt perfectly. His trainee was Madisyn. She was a shorter girl with a bright smile and overly similar to the God of Healing. They were a good match.

The God of Water's trainee, Lindsay, put out all of the torches in the room with a spray of water that forced the Goddess of Light to send light spheres to the ceiling to light everything up.

The Goddess of Wind was after that. She didn't seem too excited about her trainee, but he was excited about being down there with her. His name was Lance. He was a smaller boy and seemed frail.

The last two pairs were the Goddess of Darkness, her trainee, and Frost and I. I glanced at Frost, who leaned in close to me and whispered, "Careful, Alliana, do not strain yourself. If you need help, I will know."

He grabbed onto my arm and squeezed it tightly. Ice shattered at our feet as we appeared in the center of the colosseum. I looked at the portraits in the back and saw Frost's again. He looked strong, adhering, and cold-hearted.

"Concentrate." He whispered.

"I've never been more confident, Frost." I replied.

"I am the God of Frost." His voice echoed around the colosseum and left chills on the backs of the trainees. "Next to me is Alliana, my trainee. Her confidence and smarts will outwit and outpower *all* of you."

I took a deep breath. I closed my eyes as I attempted to muster up my power. I wasn't quite sure of my frost power, but I would have to try my best. When I opened my eyes, I felt a chill running through me. I lifted my hands over my head and saw a large clump of ice forming. I shot it up towards the ceiling. It shattered and sent shards of ice flying around the colosseum.

I felt the warmth seep into my body again as I let go of the power I was controlling. Frost's shoulder nudged mine – something that everyone else would see as an accident, but I would see as meaningful.

I barely paid attention as the Goddess of Darkness brought out her trainee. I heard her name was Victoria and she was progressing quickly with her powers. All I could think about was what Frost was thinking.

Was he proud of me? Did that pride really go that far?

After the trainees were introduced, we were to all meet at the bottom of the colosseum. Frost and I exited our balcony. Before I could move towards the stairs again, he grabbed my arm.

"Alli." His voice was firm.

"What is it?" I asked as I creased my eyebrows.

"You will get your first physical challenge today. That is way different than using your powers. I do not want you getting hurt." His eyes sparkled in the darkness. "I have helped you come this far but after today it is out of my hands."

"We talked about this already."

"But you never promised you would be careful." He retorted.

"Why does it matter? The other trainees are the least I'm

worried about." I scoffed and shook my head. "You don't need to worry about me, and I don't need to promise I'll be careful."

"Damn it, Alliana, just appease my mind. Please." He slammed his hand against the wall, accidentally pushing me up against it. I gasped and the ice formed around his hand. It crystalized the entirety of the wall while he held his hand there.

"Frost –"

"Forget it." He shook his head and turned towards the stairs. "You have five minutes to be in the colosseum." He quickly ran down them, leaving me behind.

I sighed as I touched the rapidly melting ice he left on the wall. I didn't know what was going on with him or why he was so worried, but he definitely seemed on edge.

I began down the stairs and walked straight down the hallway until I reached a set of double doors. I pushed them open. I met Frost at the sidelines of the colosseum. He had his icy exterior back on and he didn't speak a word to me.

There was a large, metal cage in the middle of the room. It had a leaderboard on the cage with names of trainees who were supposed to fight the others, I assumed.

"You can look at it." He said frigidly.

I sighed and walked towards it. It looked like my first fight was against Madisyn, the trainee of the God of Healing. Hopefully, neither of us would take this personally.

And of course, the Goddess of Fire called that Madisyn and I would be first. We were loaded into the strange, metal cage. We were both nervous and neither of us truly wanted to hurt the other. It was embarrassing I had no idea how to fight, but I assumed it would come naturally in a situation like the one I was about to be in.

She took the first step towards me and I already could tell this was going to go very horribly. She looked like she had a much stronger build than I had.

Strength isn't everything, Alli. You are smart, outwit the opponents around you.

She swung and I quickly dodged. Her hand punched into the

metal bar behind me. She grunted and I pushed myself into her. Her back hit the other side of the cage. She pushed back with all of her force, sending me on my back on the ground.

She got on top of me and, without hesitation, threw the first landed punch. The impact on my face made me cry out. The second one made me dizzy. I wasn't surprised that she was winning right now. I didn't have any knowledge of how to fight.

I lifted my legs up quickly, taking her off balance and knocking her onto her side. I scrambled to my feet and delivered a quick kick to her stomach. I could hear the wind rushing out of her lungs as she laid on her stomach.

I kicked her side next. I started to feel bad for the blows I was delivering. Were we made to be enemies?

I sat on her back and pushed her face into the hard ground below us. Her arms flailed around next to us before she caught a grip on the sleeve of my jacket. She pulled, *hard*. The sleeve ripped.

I was so shocked that she had the advantage over me for a moment and she took it. She bucked her hips, sending me flying off of her. I landed on my stomach and felt the wind being knocked out from my lungs.

Before I could even move, she was on top of me again, her hand wrapping in my hair. My eyes widened as she lifted my head and slammed it into the ground.

I had just enough time to cry out in pain before everything around me went black.

CHAPTER SIX

W aking up with a splitting headache was the least of my concerns. I couldn't open my eyes despite the effort I put into it. There was a dip in the bed where someone else sat next to me. I felt the presence of at least two people in the room.

"You need to be careful, God of Frost." There was a petite voice coming from a short distance away.

"Careful of what?" Frost was the one sitting on the bed next to me. He shifted further away from me.

"Of whatever it is she is getting you into." The woman said sternly. "It is not often we see someone who can...warm up that cold heart of yours."

"I have no clue what you are talking about." His voice became sharp. "I am simply making sure she does not fail. That is the last thing I want."

"I mean no harm, God of Frost." She replied respectfully. "But I do believe the God of Healing is on his way in to help her out. I would not be sitting there when he came in if I were you." Her footsteps sounded as dainty as her voice. She was stealthy enough to barely be heard.

Frost stood from the edge of my bed. My eyes finally fluttered open. The bright light above me made me groan.

"Hello, Alliana." Frost had somehow made it to the other side of the room. I didn't think he had any clue I heard what they were just talking about. I was curious as to who she was. She was one of the Goddesses, no doubt.

"What's up?" I chuckled softly, feeling a shooting pain in my side. "Aren't you guys supposed to be able to make this crap go away?"

"The pain?" He raised his eyebrow. "The God of Healing is on his way. You had to at least know what it felt like first."

"Trust me, I know how it feels to get my ass handed to me." I sat up despite every neuron in my body screaming at me not to.

"Physical fights are one of the most important things to learn." Frost explained. "You will have to do that again at some point."

There was a quick knock at the door before the God of Healing came in. He was a shorter man. His head was shiny and bald. He nodded at Frost before walking over to me. He glided when he walked like he was drifting through the room. Without any words, he placed his hand on my forehead. A glowing light came from his hand and a sweet, warm feeling swept through me. I took a deep breath. My headache faded away quickly.

"Your trainee may be excellent at using her power, but she needs to know how to use her strength." The God of Healing said to Frost. He took one more look at me before exiting the room.

Frost and I made eye contact. Something was swirling around in his eyes I couldn't quite figure out. I thought about the Goddess's words, wondering what she meant by them. If I asked him, there was no guarantee he wouldn't shut me out again. He was acting strange lately. He never really explained why he acted in the ways he did.

I ultimately decided it wasn't worth knowing. If it was something he wanted to explain to me, he already would have. I stood up from the bed, feeling rejuvenated. Without a word to Frost, I reached for the doorknob.

"Alli," he muttered quietly, "I knew you were awake."

"What do you mean?"

"You heard what the Goddess of Light said." He replied smoothly. "There is no need to hide it. I know you have questions. And I also know that you know I will not answer them."

"So, what was the point of you saying this?" I scoffed and turned to face him.

"So I can tell you it is *not* what you think it is. I am here to train and assist you in any way I can. Do not overthink that." His words were a hard blow on what I guess one would call my ego. I didn't think much of what he told the Goddess or what the Goddess told him. He was my mentor. What was I supposed to be overthinking?

"Don't worry, Frost, that was the last thing I was thinking about." I glanced him over with a look of disdain. "Maybe you're the one overthinking."

I left him behind in the room, with something still tugging at my heartstrings.

I found my way back to my room and placed my own hand upon the emblem. The door creaked open as it did the last time. As I was about to walk in, Madisyn walked up to me.

"Hey, Alliana!" She smiled at me. "I hope we're alright?"

"Yeah, don't worry about it." I returned a smile. "We're training. We have to do what we have to do. No hard feelings." She nodded and walked towards her room. The doors closed behind me as I walked into my room.

I flopped onto my bed and stared at the chandelier in the center of the room. I gathered a deep breath. My peace was short-lived as my doors swung open once more. I shot up and scrunched my eyebrows.

Frost walked through the door.

"You know, you should probably knock first." I sneered and crossed my arms over my chest.

"Why?" He asked obliviously.

"Frost, I..." I paused and thought about what to say next. "You know what? Never mind. Just do it."

"We must get back to the challenges." He told me. "You still have four left to do. Mine is coming up and I do believe you will excel in it."

"Can I just have ten minutes?" I groaned.

"Unfortunately, no minutes to spare. You must come now."

And that is how I ended up back on the floor of the colosseum with five of the Gods' portraits staring back at me. It looked like the next one in the order was the God of Healing. That had to be a somewhat...easy challenge. He was dressed in a long-sleeved, white shirt and a pair of black pants that were a little too short. His eyebrows were creased. He looked older, small wrinkles coming from the sides of his eyes.

I ran my fingers along the frame of the canvas before I felt myself being dragged through it. Unlike any of the other challenges, the journey to his realm was soft and sweet. I landed gently on the familiar land of my field. I breathed in the scents and felt myself relax.

The God of Healing appeared in front of me. His eyes glowed a green color as he said his riddle.

With the power of life in my palm, the way to heaven may not be so long, away with the vulnerable and more strength for the strong, and with me, the dead have no qualm.

"Alliana," He nodded at me after he said his riddle. "This challenge is unlike the others. Here, you will not have to face off with mystical creatures nor race into tornadoes; this place is about serenity. The peace you will feel here will be unparalleled in any realm, even your own."

"I understand," I replied as I watched him carefully.

"There is no room for negativity. If there is any negativity in your heart, you will not be able to pass this barrier. To pass, you must let go of all of it. Find a way to forgive and your heart will not long for any changes."

I walked towards the invisible barrier and concentrated on relieving myself of all negativity. It was a feeling so relaxing as I felt the warmth invade my body. I crossed over the border and found myself next to the God of Healing.

"Excellent, young one." He smiled. "Now, walk with me. We will discuss the trial at hand."

I walked shoulder to shoulder with the God of Healing. He was a nice man and full of wisdom.

"The whole idea behind the power to heal is the power to stay calm. Complete tranquility is needed in order to heal those we care about. Today, we will meditate and clear our minds of all thoughts. The secret to healing will come to you. The power of healing is not one to take for granted. Only those who are physically and mentally capable of handling this power can use it." He explained as we walked through the overly familiar field.

"What does physical prowess have to do with healing?"

"The road to healing is a long one. Just like in normal, everyday life. Someone must carry the burden of being the healer. For us, it is quite different. When I put my hand on your forehead in the infirmary, I felt every kick, punch, or blow Madisyn delivered to you. That is typical of my power. You can only heal the pain you can endure."

"I see." I said. "So, if someone was close to death and I couldn't bear that pain, I wouldn't be able to heal them?"

"Precisely." He nodded. "There is also a part of my power that is called regression. This is the...hard part. If we cannot heal someone who is suffering, this gives us the opportunity to help them pass faster. To relieve them of their pain in a way."

The idea of that was scary. Just as easily as you can give someone their life back, you can take it just as quickly. The God of Healing stopped in his tracks and turned to face me.

"Now, we will meditate. Come, sit."

We both sat down in the field of flowers, breathing in the beautiful aroma they left in the air. He crossed his legs as he placed his hands on his knees. I mimicked his movements.

"Now, the key to mediation is a completely blank mind. In order to successfully clear your mind, you must not think, even if it is about clearing your mind." The God of Healing took a deep breath and closed his eyes as he exhaled.

I did the same, closing my eyes. It was a lot harder than I thought it would be. Clearing your mind is something that requires patience. Unfortunately for me, patience was something I lacked.

There was a warm breeze throughout the field. The flower petals tickled my legs as they swayed in the wind. I smiled softly and inhaled deeply. On my exhale, my mind was cleared. There were no thoughts drifting endlessly through my mind.

"You are relaxed, young one." The God of Healing's voice seemed to be resonating in my mind. "This is how I feel every day, no matter what. This is the mindset you need to use the power of healing."

He and I both knew that I was ready to begin. We stood up and walked further down the field. It was a vast expansion of colorful flowers for miles. He stopped by a large sunflower that was wilting, dying.

"Now, if you concentrate, you will be able to heal this flower. It feels pain just as we do. You will feel the repercussions of its pain." He grabbed my hand, leading me to the flower. I touched it and immediately feeling an aching pain in my spine. I felt like I was being forced to hunch over. My throat became incredibly dry and I craved water.

I slowly became better as a golden glow emanated from my palm. I slowly felt the pressure alleviate from my spine as my back straightened. As I straightened, so did the flower. It continued to stretch until it was standing proudly once more.

"I will not show you regression. Regression is a dangerous part of this power and should only be attempted by those who specialize in healing." He explained. "You did very well today, Alliana. Remember to always find your peace within yourself. That is the only way you can access your true self. I have a feeling in your near future, you will need this power. You must improve yourself physically and mentally, or the person you want to protect will be lost."

And just like that, I was back in the colosseum with Frost. I frowned as I thought about who I could possibly want to protect – or who I would *need* to protect.

"What is it?" Frost asked, his eyebrows furrowed.

"Nothing…" I shook my head and met his icy blue eyes, "just something he said, that's all."

"I understand." Frost said. "He can be quite whimsical."

We sat in awkward silence for a moment and looked into each other's eyes. He wanted to say something, I knew he did. I also knew that he would never expose a side of himself that would leave him vulnerable.

I could *feel* my heart beating erratically in my chest. There was something about the depth of his blue eyes that made me lose every other thought that I had.

"There's something different about you, Frost," I whispered. "I can't put my finger on it, but you're different."

"Different from whom?"

"Everybody. Everybody else."

CHAPTER SEVEN

The idea that was Frost was so complex. Every time I took a step forward and tried to understand him. the new things I found out sent me flying ten steps backward. He, apparently, knew so much about me. That left me in the dark. *Why* and *how* did he know these things about me? Why was he so hesitant in letting me learn more about him?

I figured the next challenge would be something special, considering it was designed by Frost himself. I went from making awkward eye contact with him across the room to meeting the eyes of his portrait-self.

He was dressed in all white, almost like a jumpsuit. His emblem was proudly displayed on his shoulder. Everything about his look in this portrait depicted him as exactly what someone would think – distant, cold-hearted, and aloof.

It was odd for me, considering I rarely saw this side of him. He never came off to me as cold-hearted or distant. He was always there, *always*. He may have a snarky comment or two, but he was there nonetheless.

I would learn something about Frost in this challenge, I hoped. I looked once more from the portrait to the man standing before me. If I didn't know any better, I wouldn't even think they were the same person.

He nodded as if he knew I was looking for approval. His eyes shone with something that resembled hope. Hope for what? Hope that I make it out alive?

That was reassuring.

Setting my fears aside, I touched the canvas. This one, despite being one of the last ones, was not gentle. My body was thrown roughly into a snow pile. A blizzard raged on around me and the snowflakes were so cold they burned as they touched my skin.

My light jacket and leggings were certainly not enough to keep me warm. I stayed in my spot and waited for Frost to give me his riddle.

And almost on cue, he did exactly that.

The call of the cold and the brew of the storm, the night of the old and the beginnings of the swarm, in my winterly weather you must survive, only those with chilled hearts tend to thrive.

It was much like the water challenge in the sense of me being in the wide open. Of course, I was on land this time, so that was a nice perk.

The cold quickly began to set in. I looked down at my hands and saw they were already a bright red color. With absolutely nothing around me, I knew I had to figure out a way to get myself out of the cold.

I used my power over frost before, but never in a way to prevent cold. It was like my brain wasn't working. The cold was sending me into overdrive while also shutting me down.

"Frost," I gasped, watching as the puff of air escaped my lips, "where do I start?"

I wasn't really expecting an answer, but it wasn't just the snow that stung. His lack of response proved to me that I was on my own. I had to be on my own. This was his lesson I couldn't rely on him. He wouldn't be there for me forever. At least, he didn't *say* he would be.

Despite barely being able to concentrate, I clenched my fists. I could barely feel my fingers now. I closed my eyes, waving my hand in an upward motion. A disgruntled sort of igloo formed in front of me.

It wasn't *exactly* what I was picturing when I imagined it, but at least it was somewhere to go. I quickly crawled inside of it. It had to be below freezing outside, as I figured it would be. Being in the igloo, after outside, felt like a dream. It wasn't exactly warm, but it was warmer than the open air.

I curled into a fetal position and leaned against the wall of the igloo. There seemed to be no point to this challenge other than to freeze to death. I guess I would have to wait and see what Frost had in store for me.

I must have been in there for hours. I thought and wondered what I could possibly do. When I came out of the igloo, the blizzard had subsided and night had fallen. I started to walk, even though I was interrupted by a loud howl.

My blood ran cold. I couldn't imagine that being good.

I saw a wolf coming from the darkness of the horizon. He had a great white coat and incredibly vibrant blue eyes. I took a step backward but the wolf came and sat in front of me. His tongue lolled out of his mouth as he sat, looking at me with a tilted head.

"Hey there, uh...wolfy." I took another step back. "Didn't mean to come onto your territory or anything."

He stood and shook to get the snow off of his fur. He turned around and started walking in the direction he came from. He stopped after moving a few feet and turned back around to look at me.

"Frost, if I follow this wolf and die, remember this is *your* challenge," I said as I looked up to the sky. I sighed loudly and decided to follow the wolf.

We walked straight for what felt like forever before I saw a drift of fire smoke wading into the stars. I felt a rush of excitement coursing through me as I thought of the warmth of a fire. The wolf led me straight to it.

Sitting at the fire was Frost. There were four logs set up around a makeshift fire pit. He didn't seem cold at all as he stared into the fire. The wolf walked over to Frost and sat down. I walked to the log next to the one Frost was on and sat.

"Welcome, Alliana." Frost patted the wolf's head. "I see you have met Gelum. He picks the people he helps out."

"You named a wolf?"

"Gelum has been my best friend – my only friend – for some time now. Even on the coldest of nights, he never strays from my side. I am starting to think it is the fire that keeps him here."

Frost smiled a genuine smile at his wolf. My heart twisted into several different kinds of knots just watching him interact with Gelum.

"You never told me about him." I mentioned as I admired the obvious connection he had with the canine.

"Not many people know about him, actually. I have spent many years out here, Alli. There are things here even I cannot explain. The storm does whatever it wants." His eyes were almost an exact match for Gelum's. The icy blue color was something to be jealous of.

"I - Frost…"

"You do not have to say anything, Alliana. In fact, there are some things I need to discuss with you. At least I know we are alone and in solidarity here in my realm." He met my eyes with a small twinkle in his that I rarely got to see.

He looked down at his hands before looking to the sky.

"The stars are breathtaking." He pointed out one of the constellations. "Ursa Major. The skies here are just…absolutely perfect. You know, the Iroquois created a myth behind this constellation. Ursa Major is a great bear, hunted by three hunters. It is truly fascinating how each culture, religion…anyone really, can come up with ideas and stories like that. I truly envy the creativity of those people." He never looked away from the sky.

I followed his gaze to find the constellation he was speaking of. There were *millions* of stars dotted across the sky and the full moon lit them up. I could never remember seeing the night sky look like this.

"Alli," he began, "you are one of those people I admire. Your strength and tenacity are unparalleled, and in spite of all the things you went through as a young child, you persevered. I cannot even begin to imagine all of what you have been through."

"All of that led me straight to you, Frost." I replied quietly as I looked down from the sky to my feet. "Everything that's happened to me led me right where I needed to be."

"I have looked out for you almost your entire life. Never, not even once, did I have to intervene." He chuckled softly. "You sure knew how to prove me and all of the others wrong."

A small stretch of silence ensued. I wasn't exactly sure what to say to him, but I wanted him to know that I understood what he was saying. The fire crackled a couple of times. Sparks flew into the air along with the smoke.

"Alliana..." Frost sighed, "you are a danger to me. An incredible danger I cannot escape."

"What do you mean?" I questioned.

"Up until now, it has been Gelum, the snow, and I. Welcoming you here has been...nothing short of interesting. I...I do not want you to leave. I want you to stay here. With me, that is."

"Frost, this is just one of the challenges." I responded. "I can't stay here."

"I know." He suspired. "If only it were that easy. I remember when I first came here when I was younger. I never imagined I would be where I am now. The cold has become a comfort, as have you, in a way. We must not feel *comfortable* with each other, Alli."

Without another word, he stood from his spot. He reached his hand out to me. I took it. For a few short moments, nothing happened. He looked from our hands to my eyes, then back to our hands. I felt a tug. Not like I was being pulled into another realm, but like I was being pulled into Frost.

Before I knew what was happening, Frost's arms were wrapped around me. His grip was tight as he rested his head on top of mine. I was absolutely speechless. Without a second thought, my arms followed suit.

Here we were, locked in an embrace in the middle of what was supposed to be his challenge. There was nothing – and I mean absolutely *nothing* – challenging about this. He was soft and he smelled like the fire that burned beside us.

His fingers curled lightly into the fabric on the back of my shirt. It was a small gesture but it meant the world.

The area around us started to spin. Soon enough, we were back in the warmth of the colosseum. His arms were still wrapped tightly around me. Only when he realized where we were did he finally let go.

I wouldn't describe this feeling as...empty, but I certainly felt unfulfilled once he let go.

My heart was pounding in my chest. I didn't know what that meant or what I was even supposed to do. He made my palms sweat and an aching feeling form in my chest.

"We should...we should come back to these tomorrow, Alliana." He turned to walk into the corridor. "If you take the first right, you should arrive at your room."

"Frost, wait!"

He turned around to look at me with impatience setting in. He was running again, and I didn't know if it was from me or from what he was thinking.

"Can you walk me there? Please?" My voice was smaller than I liked, but there was no taking the words back once they were out in the open.

"I do not think that is a good idea." He sighed. "But I will do it anyway."

I walked over to him and felt a chill run up my spine. My fingers felt numb as I adjusted to the heat. We walked to my room in silence. Thousands of words were running through my mind.

"Alliana, this is a dangerous world." He whispered as we made it to my door. "Whatever happened today, keep it to yourself." There was an urgency in his words. His eyes were wide and for the first time ever, I saw the vulnerability sparkling in them.

He may not be technically human, but he sure felt the same emotions as one. That on its own had to be tremendously scary. He was this great, powerful being, and suddenly someone just walked into his life and made him feel.

All I did was blink and he was gone. I took a deep breath and exhaled it quickly. I shook my head while turning towards my door. I placed my hand on the emblem and entered the room as the doors swung open.

They closed behind me and I climbed onto my bed. There was something so strange about whatever I was feeling. I *wanted* to talk to Frost. I *wanted* to be by him, in his realm, sitting by the fire.

There are things people wanted in this world and they will never receive them.

At this point, I was beginning to think that was happening with Frost. That was strange, considering I didn't even *know* what I wanted from him. I saw a side of him in his realm I was never able to see before. He openly shared that side with me.

He was holding something back and I don't think even he knew what it was.

CHAPTER EIGHT

I walked into the colosseum, expecting it to be empty once again. Instead, I found every one of the trainees was sitting at a table. Madisyn smiled when she saw me and beckoned for me to sit next to her.

I sat down, Madisyn to my right, and Apolonia to my left. The whole table was chatting away and it was safe to say I was lost. The doors swung open behind us.

The Gods and Goddesses walked in one-by-one. The Goddesses were in dresses resembling ball gowns and the Gods, nowhere near as dressed up, were in slacks and a white shirt. It was easy to ignore everyone walking in as I awaited Frost's entrance.

He walked in second to last. His eyes scanned over the table until he met mine. I looked away only when I felt a nudge in my side.

"I wonder what they're so dressed up for." She whispered.

"I don't know." I shrugged. "Those dresses are gorgeous though."

"Whatever this is, I don't think it's good." The boy I recognized as Derek said. "The Goddess of Fire never said this was a part of the training"

"Frost didn't say anything was going on today." I said. I found him settling into the front of the room.

"Why do you call him Frost?" Madisyn asked. "Aren't they like...super strict about that?"

"He used to be, but I just did it anyway." I replied. "He hasn't said anything for a while."

"Jeez, I think the God of Healing would send me right home if I gave him a nickname." Madisyn chuckled. "The God of Frost must be really nice. He seems...standoffish."

"He can be. I learned a lot about him in his challenge yesterday." I told her.

"His challenge was so hard! I swear, I almost froze to death!" Maximo interjected. "Fighting off whatever that giant ass thing was...that was tough! He sure knew how to put us to the test."

"What giant thing?" I asked with a frown.

"You know, he was like an abominable snowman but huge and made of ice! He was not easy to defeat at all." Derek's eyes were wide as he described the challenge. "It was pretty sick, though."

I looked down at my hands. Frost's challenge was so different for me. I remembered what he said about keeping things to myself, so I decided to stop talking.

Madisyn was an intricate person. Despite beating me up a few days ago, she was one of the nicest people I'd ever met. She was funny, sweet, and certainly didn't take anything from anyone. Maximo was the same; he was funny and a little on the shyer side than Madisyn was.

Derek, on the other hand, was a whole other being to talk about. He had an arrogant persona that was almost hard to get along with. He was clashing with the rest of the group.

"Alright, I think we have kept you waiting long enough." The Goddess of Fire's voice echoed from the other side of the room. Her dress was a bright red. The earrings dangling from her ears revealed her emblem.

"You are probably wondering what this is about." Frost's voice continued. "Up until now, you have done each challenge on your own. You each have two challenges left. After this next challenge, you will be going in as a group into the last challenge."

"The last challenge is the Goddess of Darkness' and mine." The Goddess of Light began. "In the past, ours has proven nearly impossible to win on your own, so all eight of you will go in together."

"Teamwork and *hard* work will get you out of that canvas."

The Goddess of Darkness said next. "It is whether or not you use each other properly that will determine if you make it out."

"Today, you will all complete your next challenge, but this one will be alone. You will be alone with your mentor before you embark on the next, incredibly important challenge. Prove yourselves worthy and you will make it to the Light and Darkness challenge." The God of Water continued.

"Now, we must disperse. First up for this challenge is Alliana, trainee to the God of Frost." The Goddess of Wind's eyes narrowed at me through the crowd. Of *course,* I was first. The Fire challenge was not really one I was looking forward to.

"Good luck, Alliana." Madisyn whispered before filing out of the room with the rest of the trainees.

The doors slammed behind the crowd as they left. Frost and I were the only ones in the room. He walked towards me with a purpose.

"Is everything alright?" He asked with a frown.

"Your challenge. Did you change it for me?" I replied in a hushed whisper.

"What do you mean?"

"Derek and Maximo were telling me about your challenge and it was nothing like what I experienced, Frost." A look of disdain fell upon me. "How do I make myself worthy of this power if you make it easier for me?"

"That was not the point of changing it, Alli, trust me. I changed it because I wanted some time to talk to you. A place where nobody would be listening." He looked around cautiously.

"You really don't trust people here?"

"No, and neither should you. None of the trainees or the other Gods have what is best for you in mind. You would be smart to remember that." He said vehemently while taking a step closer to me. There was barely enough space between us for me to turn without brushing against him.

"Um, Frost..." I cleared my throat. "I think I should do this challenge." My words were barely escaping my lips.

"Of course." He nodded and took a step back. "Just be wary,

Alliana. They do not have your best interest in mind. They never have and they never will."

I turned away and walked towards the second to last canvas. The Goddess of Fire was very obviously not someone to mess with. She was stern and, no pun intended, fiery. I couldn't even begin to imagine what her challenge would be like.

"Good luck, Alliana. You must come back."

※ ※ ※ ※ ※ ※ ※

I barely recalled touching the canvas at all. I was now standing in an empty field with a small house sitting in front of me. The Goddess of Fire stood in front of the house as her dress billowed in the soft wind.

Her eyes glowed a deep red as she recited her riddle.

Within the force of scorching flames, I am not the only one you will meet, close your eyes and play my games, your dearest love is in the heat.

Well, that was ominous. The Goddess of Fire turned towards the house and lifted her hand. The building burst into flames. I felt a physical pull towards the building and worry settled into me.

I didn't know who, but I knew that someone I cared about was in the burning building and unable to get out by themselves. The Goddess of Fire disappeared.

I ran towards the house. Every one of my fears subsided as I felt the pull and the connection with whoever was in there.

Your dearest love is in the heat. As far as I knew, I loved nobody except for my mother and possibly a close friend. Love was such a foreign concept for me. I never experienced it.

My first instinct was to run up the stairs. I halted as soon as I stepped through the front door. The smoke was everywhere and my eyes were beginning to water. I coughed and tried to think while I ran.

I got down on the floor and crawled up the stairs. My throat felt like sandpaper already. I made it up the stairs, turning in one of the rooms.

The ceiling cracked above me as it crashed down onto the floor. The floor split in two. I rolled quickly onto my back. I sighed in relief just a bit too soon. The floor cracked beneath me, and before I could even think to move, I fell through!

My back slammed against the dining room table. I cried out in pain while clenching my eyes shut. The flames roared around me. I looked around, searching for where my *dearest love* might be.

Black began to border my vision as I sat up. My head started pounding but I knew I had to carry on. I had to make it to the end! There was a room off to the side. It was the only room left that hadn't succumbed to the flames.

I slid off the table and onto my feet. I grunted quietly at the shooting pain in my legs. I limped over to the doorway and stopped in my tracks.

This couldn't be right! There was no way this was happening! My heart skipped a beat. All this time I wondered what this feeling I'd experienced was with Frost. Little did I know, it would take this challenge to figure it out. My throat felt tight. Was that feeling actually...love?

There Frost sat, knocked out in a chair. His right wrist was tied down with a thick rope. Jumping into action, I squatted down by the arm of the chair to see what the knot looked like. I looked up at his oddly peaceful face.

"Frost, wake up." I shook him. "I'm gonna get you out of here."

I clenched my eyes shut and tried to think of anything that could help me. I opened my palm and concentrated.

I then opened my eyes and saw exactly what I wanted. I made a ridiculously sharp ice shard to cut the rope. It was tight around his wrist. I took a second glance at the rapidly melting shard. It was now or never.

"Sorry, Frost, this might hurt just a little." I quickly shoved the shard underneath the rope. I started shaking as I saw his blood trail down his arm and drip onto the floor. I yanked upwards and the rope instantly snapped in two. I threw the ice shard as I heard the building creak around us.

He needed to wake up and he needed to wake up, *now*! The

63

building was going to give at any second. With not much else I could think of doing, I wound back and slapped him as hard as I could.

His blue eyes shot open with a groan escaping his lips. It only took him a second to come to as he realized what was happening around us.

He got up from his seat and wobbled as he stood. I grabbed him while putting his arm over my shoulder.

"We have to go." I practically dragged him from the building. The front door seemed so far away although the house was tiny. He was basically dead weight at this point. I heard the house violently creak once more.

With a loud grunt, I used all of my strength to push both of us out of the door. As soon as we made it out, the house crumbled behind us. I fell to the ground and took Frost with me. Rain started pouring from the sky. I looked over to Frost while breathing sharply. His wrist was still bleeding from when I cut the rope.

I drew in a long breathe and shut my eyes. I grabbed his hand as I shook and willed all the thoughts out of my head. I opened my eyes and saw a bright, golden color glowing from my hands once more.

I felt something sharp slice against my wrist. I quietly gasped as I waited for it to feel better. It slowly recovered as I watched as his wound seal itself up as well.

"Alli," he whispered. His hand came up to cup my cheek, "You know the truth now."

My eyes watered as I looked at him. I glanced behind me and saw the Goddess of Fire standing next to Frost. There was a dark, terrified look on his face as he watched the scene play out in front of him. I looked back to the ground to see the Frost in my challenge slowly fading away.

I matched the look in Frost's eyes with my own.

There was no explanation for this.

CHAPTER NINE

Before I knew what happened, I was back in my bedroom. The curtains had been drawn on the window and a bright light fluttered through it. I sat up, still feeling sore from the challenge. I didn't know how I ended up back in here.

There was a knock at the door. I stood and walked over to it slowly. I pulled the set of doors open and saw Madisyn and Maximo standing at the door.

"Oh, hey guys." I cleared my throat. "What's going on?"

"You've been out for like a whole day." Madisyn said. "We were worried and just wanted to check on you." I opened the door wider so they could come in. I sat on the edge of my bed.

"Wow, this room is so cool." Maximo looked around. "Mine is kinda...earthy." He shrugged.

"Wait..." I looked between the two of them. "A whole day? Where's Frost?"

"We just left a meeting, actually. The God of Frost wasn't there, though." Maximo explained. "The God of Earth said he had some business to take care of today. I guess he'll be back tomorrow or something. But we're about to start the light and darkness challenge, so we came to get you."

"Oh, thanks, Maximo." I gave him a warm smile even though the worry clouded my mind. What was it that Frost needed to do?

"You can call me Max." He replied.

"We should get going, though. They want to start soon." Madisyn interjected. "We can talk on the way."

"Alright. Let me change really quick. I smell like a bonfire."

❋ ❋ ❋ ❋ ❋ ❋ ❋

The three of us made it down to the colosseum quickly after I changed. We sat with Derek. The other trainees sat amongst themselves. The Gods and Goddesses in front of us were giving us instructions, but all I could think about was what Frost could possibly be doing.

"Do you guys want to stick together in there?" Madisyn leaned into our inner circle. "It would probably be easier if we combined our powers in there."

"I think that's a good idea." I offered.

"I'll carry the team, guys." Derek smirked.

Another one of the trainees started to walk over to our group. Apolonia was the trainee of the Goddess of Light. She was a very sweet girl. She had long hair that drifted to the middle of her back. I didn't think anyone was able to *look* nice until I saw her.

"Do you mind if I join you guys?" She asked softly. Madisyn scooted closer to me and Max scooted the other way to make a spot for her. She sat next to them.

"We're always welcoming new people." Max smiled at her.

"I figured the more power we have in this challenge, the better it will be for us." Apolonia replied.

The five of us were gathered in the group, while Lindsay, Lance, and Victoria were off in their own small group.

"The groups you have formed will be who you go into the challenge with. There are certain strategies you will need to make it through. Derek, your group will go first." The Goddess of Fire said Derek's name but her eyes stared deep into my soul.

There was something wrong. I didn't know exactly what, but I felt it.

"See, guys? *My* team." Derek said.

"Yeah, whatever. Let's get going." I rolled my eyes and walked towards the portrait. We all looked at each other once more and then touched the canvas one by one.

Wherever I ended up, it was pitch black. I put my hand out, walking forward a little bit. There was a thud against the ground as someone else came through the canvas.

"Ow," the familiar voice of Maximo moaned, "why is it so dark in here? Why is the damn floor so hard?" I couldn't help but chuckle as he stood. One by one, the other three came through the canvas effortlessly.

"I think you were the only one that had a hard time, Max." I teased him with a smile on my face.

"I-." He started to reply, but was cut off when we heard a deep grumble echo off the walls.

"Oh, you've got to be kidding me." I groaned. "Derek, Apolonia, we're gonna need to see."

"Right," Apolonia murmured. A small ball of pure light began to form in her hands and lit everyone up with a slight glow.

"Is that as bright as it gets?" Derek asked with a disdained look on his face. "You should make it -!" Derek was cut off when whatever was growling jumped on him.

Whatever it was *looked* human, but certainly was not. Without even thinking, I jumped onto its back in an attempt to pull it off of Derek. It shrieked and clawed at my arms. I cried out in pain as its claws ripped into the skin of my arm. I refused to let go. It backed up into the wall and slammed me into it.

I wailed in pain and held on to it as it smashed me into the wall again. The ground below us rumbled.

"Alliana! Let go!" Max shouted. I released its shoulders and fell to the ground with a thud. A piece of the ground lifted from the rest. It flew into the creature at a high speed, crushing it against the wall behind us.

I breathed heavily while I let my head fall against the wall.

"Alli, are you okay?" Madisyn ran over to me and grabbed my arms. The white fabric I was wearing was now stained red. Blood gushed from the wounds the creature had inflicted.

"As okay as I can be." I chuckled weakly. I watched as Madisyn closed her eyes. She opened them again. Her eyes were bright, vibrant green. She gripped my wrists tightly. A familiar golden glow resonated from her hands. She took a sharp intake of breath and scrunched up her face in a response to the pain.

I breathed slowly, feeling at peace within myself as my wounds began to close up. Madisyn let go once I was healed. She breathed a sigh of relief as she stood and held her hand out to me to help me stand.

I took it. Apolonia's light became a bit brighter. I could finally see our surroundings. Besides the big hole that was now in the floor because of Max, the rest of the floor was a deep, black marble. The walls were exactly the same.

"Not to put a damper on this, guys…" Apolonia muttered, "but I think we're in a maze."

We all looked around, hoping to disprove her theory. She sent another ball of light down the hallway. It showed different branches of hallways. The ball of light traveled so far down the hallway, it disappeared from sight.

"Welcome, young trainees." The voice echoed off the walls. It belonged to the Goddess of Darkness. "You are here in my part of the challenge. You will be encountered by many different creatures of darkness, so be prepared. They have strict orders to try and kill whoever comes to their territory."

"Oh, isn't that great." Derek scoffed and wiped the blood from the small cut on his cheek.

"Now, in my part of the challenge," The Goddess of Light interjected, "you must remember that light will always guide you through darkness. Light and darkness work together, forever and always."

Then, in sync, they finally delivered us our riddle.

Within one, you will find the other, we work hand in hand, both together. You can't run from us, you can't hide, deep within your soul, we do preside.

"We can't possibly go through *all* of these corridors." Madisyn grumbled. "We'll be in here for decades."

"I wonder if there's a way we can just climb to the top and

look." Max frowned while walking over to the marble walls. "Yeah, these are gonna be a little hard to climb."

"Well, according to the God of Frost, Alliana knows how to do it all, doesn't she?" Derek tilted his head as he looked at me.

"Come on, Derek, don't start." Madisyn warned him.

"Well, if she's so *great*, why doesn't she lead the way?" He asked sarcastically. "I wouldn't be surprised if the God of Frost helped you cheat through all of your challenges."

"Where the hell is that coming from?" I jeered.

"Yeah, you know he's not allowed to do that."

"The Gods aren't allowed to do a *lot* of stuff he just does anyway." Derek retorted. "I mean, the Goddess of Fire said the God of Frost was in Alliana's burning building."

I froze in my spot. I felt everyone's eyes on me.

"Derek, now is literally the worst time." I began.

"You know she just saved your freakin' life, right?" Max intervened. He stepped in between Derek and I. "Obviously she knows more than you do, or you wouldn't have needed her to save you."

"I had it under control!" Derek took a step closer to Max.

"No, you didn't! You sat in the corner like a baby instead of helping Alli. She could've died trying to protect you. What was the point of you even being in this group if you were just going to be an ass?" Max countered Derek's step with one of his own. They were now only a few inches apart.

"Stop, both of you!" I tried to grab Max's shoulder.

"They're breaking all of the rules and all of you are just *fine* with that?" Derek asked. Max rolled his eyes and, without hesitation, delivered a punch right to Derek's left cheek.

Derek doubled back before launching himself at Max. The two were throwing blow after blow. Madisyn and Apolonia ran to them and attempted to pull Max and Derek apart.

Madisyn pulled Derek away first. Both girls moved in front of the two angry boys. Derek shook Madisyn away while attempting to move towards Max again.

"That's enough!" My voice echoed against the walls as I lifted my hand. A giant ice wall formed between the four other trainees. They all stopped and looked at me.

"Alli, I was just..." Max began.

"I know, thank you, but that's enough. We have a challenge to complete. We can duke out our disagreements later. For now, we need to get moving before we get attacked again." I turned around and walked down the hall. Apolonia nodded and followed me. The ball of glowing light followed her as she walked.

Max, Apolonia, and Madisyn walked in front while I lingered behind, waiting to find Derek. He caught up to me and gave me a glance.

"Just so you know," I gave him a stern look, "regardless of what you were told, I worked my ass off to be here right now. I've jumped into endless holes and, hell, even into a tornado. So, before you try to tell me *how* I got here, maybe you should take a look and evaluate yourself."

I left him standing there, unsure of how to respond. I caught up with the other three and fit in between Max and Madisyn.

"Thanks, Max, for standing up for me." I nudged him gently.

"Any time." He nodded. "But...is it true? Was the God of Frost in your burning house?"

"Yes, he was. It doesn't matter and it never has." I told him. "I hope you guys don't think differently of me."

"I mean, honestly? I think that's pretty sick. Wherever he is, I'm sure he's proud of you and how far you've come." Max replied.

"Yeah, agreed." Madisyn smiled at me.

We approached the first set of corridors. We could go left, right, or straight. I recalled a similar part of the water challenge that made me choose the direction. Although at that time, I probably channeled that power because Frost was waiting for me down the hallway.

"Wait." I told them. "I can figure out which way to go."

I closed my eyes and focused all my energy. When I opened my eyes, I was met with a sparkling light trailing down the corridor to my left.

"This way."

They followed me without hesitation. Thankfully, we were not doing the challenge on our own. It was nice to finally have a support system. Derek was straggling a few feet behind us. He refused to join the group.

A wind drifted through the corridor. It sounded like something extremely large took a great breath.

"Hey, guys," Apolonia gulped, "that doesn't sound too good."

"No, it doesn't." Madisyn confirmed as we hesitantly walked forward.

The corridor suddenly branched off into an unbelievably large room. And, of course, in the middle was either the biggest lizard I'd ever seen in my life or a dragon.

"*Please* don't tell me that's what I think it is." Madisyn groaned hopefully.

"What are the chances it's a stuffed animal?" Max offered. He earned a glare from all three of us girls.

"You're not serious, right?" I asked with a raised eyebrow.

"Okay, maybe that's wishful thinking." Max shrugged. "But I sure as hell don't want to fight that thing."

"We'll have to try and sneak past it." Apolonia suggested. "There's no other way to avoid fighting it." She lamented and ran her fingers through her hair.

"I can distract it while you guys run across." Derek offered. "I do have fire powers, after all."

"No, that's too risky. What if you don't make it?" Madisyn interjected

"Then I don't make it." Derek replied firmly. "I sincerely doubt the Goddess of Darkness programmed her *dragon* to sleep when intruders are in the room."

"Why don't we make a cage?" Max said. "I can literally make it out of this marble these walls are made of."

"He might wake up in the process." Derek warned.

"I guess it's us against this thing, so the girls can get across." Max held his hand out to Derek. Derek nodded and shook it.

The two boys were literally fist fighting just half an hour ago. Derek looked at me and gave me a small nod. The ground began to rumble. Bars of marble shot from the ground. The three of us – Madisyn, Apolonia, and I – started to run across the room. Just before the bars completed at the top, the dragon awoke with a loud screech.

It spread its wings and crushed the bars around it. I looked back at Max, who gestured at me to keep running. We were halfway across now. The dragon found us not even a moment later.

"Hey there, you overgrown gecko! Look over here." Derek confidently walked to the middle of the room. "I'm right here! Come get me!"

The dragon let out a roar as its attention was redirected towards Derek. The three of us finally made it to the other side. We watched as Max and Derek attempted to make their way across. Max tore a piece of the wall off and threw it onto the dragon's wing.

It shrieked in agony as the large piece of marble tore right through its wing. Taking its anger out on Derek, a large flame billowed from its mouth right towards him.

He held up both of his arms to shield himself. A puff of flame appearing before him. The dragon's flame bounced off of his and hit the opposite wall. Max threw another piece of marble as he made his way over to where we stood.

"Derek, hurry!" Max called as he passed through to the other side.

Derek bolted, taking the fastest path. That, of course, was straight under the dragon. In its daze, it barely realized where Derek went. It was going to fall and the panic was setting in on Derek's face.

I lifted my hand and willed all of my power out in one movement. A giant sheet of ice formed under the dragon to support its weight until Derek safely cleared the room. He quickly made it over to us and we all barreled away from the dragon.

"That...was ridiculous." Derek panted. "But pretty cool, I have to admit."

Another quieter screech echoed against the walls, similar to the first beast we faced.

"Not again," Apolonia groaned as she looked around to find the source. We took the next right and continued straight for a moment.

Suddenly, I was forced against the wall. I grunted as the air knocked right out of me. I saw the face of the creature. Whatever it was had such pure black eyes, I could see my reflection in them. Its hand held me against the wall by my throat. Its long nails dug uncomfortably into my skin.

I reached up and wrapped my fingers around his throat. I started gasping for air as I closed my eyes. Once they opened again, I saw my eyes glowing a bright, blue color within the reflection. Spears of ice shot from his eyes and mouth. A gurgled scream ripped from his throat before he released me and crumbled to the ground.

The other trainees looked at me with an uncertain gaze in their eyes.

"I have a feeling we're close to the end." I told them. "This way."

We quickly made our way down the corridor and saw a set of double doors at the end of the hallway.

"Uh...yeah, and we better make it quick." Max said. We all looked in the same directions and saw hundreds of those creatures barreling towards us.

"Run!" Derek yelled.

Within a split second, we all bolted towards the doors. Against one? I liked our chances. Against *hundreds*? Not so much.

We reached the doors with seconds to spare. Derek and Max pulled them open. Madisyn, Apolonia, and I made it through. We turned around to make sure Derek and Max made it too. We slammed the doors closed together. All of us breathing heavily.

We turned around and were blinded by the exceedingly bright light of the sun. Once our eyes adjusted to the light, we were met with our mentors – the Goddess of Fire, the Goddess of Light, the God of Earth, and the God of Healing. My heart sank when I didn't see Frost.

This wasn't like him. He wouldn't miss my *last* challenge if he could help it. I knew something was wrong and now I had to do everything in my power to find him.

"Congratulations, trainees." The Goddess of Fire stepped forward. "You have successfully completed your training."

CHAPTER TEN

A s I went to bed that night, all I could think about was Frost. There had to be something I could do. I was done with my training. I should be excited about that. All I knew was Frost should be there with me. He should have been waiting at the end of the Light and Darkness challenge for me, just as everyone else was for their trainees.

I sat up in my bed and wondered why I was still sitting there. If I could look for Frost, if I could *find* Frost, maybe he would explain why he wasn't there for me. The only logical reason was that he was in danger.

Frost was a lot of things, but unreliable was not one.

I pulled the blankets off of me, scrambling out of bed to find Madisyn's room. I knocked on the door, trying to be as quiet as possible. A set of doors opened that did not belong to Madisyn. I looked over and saw Maximo walking out of his room.

"Alli, what are you doing?" He asked quietly while rubbing his eyes. "It's like, two in the morning."

"You come too, actually, I need to talk to you and Madisyn." I ushered him over to Madisyn's door. I knocked again. This time, her doors swung open. She saw us standing there, then left her door open and walked back to her bed.

"Do you two know how late it is?" She grumbled and wrapped herself in her blankets. "What's going on?"

"You two are the only two I can trust." I told them. "I need help. *Frost* needs your help." Madisyn grimaced.

"What's going on with him? It was unlike him to miss the end of our challenge." She had a sympathetic glow in her eyes. Max put his hand on my shoulder.

"That's what I was thinking. I...I know this sounds crazy, but I think the Goddess of Fire did something to him. She kept *looking* at me every time I stopped to look for Frost." I explained to them as my heart sunk in my chest.

"Well, if the Goddess of Fire has anything to do with it...that means he has to be here, right?" Max offered with a hopeful tone in his voice.

"Best case scenario, yes." I nodded. "Worst case scenario? He's stuck somewhere deep inside her realm."

"And it would be next to impossible to find him." Madisyn gulped while confirming my worst fear. The three of us sat there for a moment before I thought of anything else to say.

"I would like to say I consider you guys as my friends. I know I can trust you two. Frost means everything to me. I didn't really know it until it was too late, but he can't be gone." After I said that, I looked at my feet in sorrow.

"Do you really think we'd let you do this on your own?" Madisyn chuckled as she slipped the blanket from her shoulders. "The only way we're going to find out if he's still here is if we look for him. What better time to do that than in the middle of the night?"

Both of them gave me a wide smile. I returned it easily. There was something so...heartwarming about this. Neither of them knew me very well, but they believed in me so much that they were willing to potentially risk their lives.

"Thank you, guys." I said with tears welling in my eyes. "You don't know how much this means to me."

"You'd do the same for us in the blink of an eye." Maximo replied. "It's really no question."

We went to our given rooms to change. We were going to find Frost tonight, no matter what it took. He was missing for too long already. The idea of the Goddess of Fire hurting him broke my heart into pieces.

I was now used to the all-white outfit I was supposed to wear at all times. It matched Frost's usual attire. I looked at myself in the mirror for a moment before I straightened my jacket out. I brushed my fingers over the emblem before I walked back out of my room.

"Should we split up?" Max asked. "We'd definitely cover way more area in a shorter time."

"What happens if we find Frost and we're alone?" Madisyn pointed out. "I'm not exactly looking to face the wrath of the Goddess of Fire all on my own."

"Solid point." Max nodded. "Where to first?"

"Well, it has to be somewhere we haven't been before, right? If he was somewhere like that, we would've seen him already." I said as I mapped out the place in my head.

"There's that one hallway nobody goes down. The God of Healing said it was just a dead-end, though." Madisyn replied.

"Let's head that way, then." I nodded.

Wherever you are, Frost, we're coming for you. I thought, looking up at the ceiling. I hoped he could hear me, regardless of how illogical that was.

As soon as we turned down that hallway, we were confronted by the Goddess of Light.

"And where might you three be going?" She asked softly. Her eyes met mine with a sympathetic tint to them. She knew exactly why we were there and she was proof that Frost was just a little bit ahead.

"I think you know." I stepped in front of Max and Madisyn. "And the only reason you're asking is because you're not going to send us back to our rooms."

"The God of Frost and I have been friends for...centuries, Alliana." She replied coolly. "While I wish nothing but his success, you hinder that greatly."

I gulped, afraid of what she was going to say to me next. She was going to tell me to forget what I thought was happening and go back. Frost would be returned in a couple of days and he would be colder than ever.

"But I can't let him lose something I know he wants more than anything. I will let you pass, but only you. He will be in his most vulnerable form and you will probably see some things that will make you want to intervene." She remained completely calm. "He broke just about...every rule we have by falling for you, Alliana. Do *not* make him regret that."

She stepped aside and eyed the other trainees. They nodded and then stood back. I walked with her to the end of the hallway, where she drew a symbol on the wall.

"Remember what I said, Alliana." She said quietly as the wall faded away. "Do not do anything to compromise the opportunity I have given you."

"Thank you," I nodded and walked past the wall. It sealed behind me. I was on a balcony that towered over a building looking like the colosseum I did my training in. There was one difference: the platform in the middle.

I teared up as I covered my mouth to keep myself from making a noise. I ducked below the bars so I could see through them. A long metal chain hung from the ceiling all the way to the platform. The cuffs on the end were attached to Frost's wrists.

He sat on his knees with his arms chained above his head. His hair was messy and his shirt had rips in it. He was breathing heavily while his body leaned over to one side. His arms were carrying the entirety of his body weight. The double doors on the other end of the room swung open.

I recognized the Goddess of Wind. Anger began to swirl within me as the doors slammed behind her.

"Oh, dear." She muttered, clicking her tongue at the sight of him. "What a shame, the mighty God of Frost finally being brought to his knees."

"Do me a favor." He grumbled. "Kill me before you give me a lecture."

"Please, you know as well as I do we are not going to kill you." The Goddess of Wind laughed. "It is pathetic, really. You did all of this because you fell for your *trainee*? Of all people?"

"She, at her worst, is better than two of you at your best." He growled at her weakly. "You will *never* take that from me." My heart wrenched as I watched him struggle against his chains.

"I should have killed her that day." She sighed. "I could have saved you. I could have prevented this from ever happening."

"What do you mean?" He lowered his voice.

"You do not know?" She chuckled. "That is honestly adorable. Naïve, but adorable. You saw it in the wind challenge for her. That tornado that ran through her village was not *natural*. It was sent to kill *her*."

"You are an insufferable witch." Frost snarled between his teeth. "Do you enjoy hurting other people?"

"More than you know." She replied comfortably. "Especially anyone who tries to take you from me."

"You never had me, Goddess of Wind. There was never anything for us." He quickly said to her. "You are delusional."

"I have known you for so long." She shook her head slowly. "It is a shame we have to do this to you."

The Goddess of Wind turned away from Frost and took her exit from the room. Just as I thought I would have the opportunity to save him, the Goddess of Fire entered after her.

I could barely stand to watch this. I wanted to help him. Every muscle in my body ached at staying still.

"This *is* a shame, God of Frost." The Goddess of Fire shook her head slowly at the sight before her. "All it takes for you to get out of this is to let her go." I watched as his fists clenched with a look of disgust appearing on his face.

"You have no idea what you are even speaking of." He told her. "You *all* are just terrified Alliana will beat you. You have never seen someone with her power before."

"Yes, but without her mentor, she will never learn how to control it." The Goddess of Fire said suavely while walking towards him and grabbing his face with her hand. "Is it not the most...despicable thing you have ever heard? Your trainee has caused nothing but trouble for you, but you want to protect her. You are...daring. Foolish, I would say."

"I would rather be in here for a millennium before I let you put your filthy hands on her." He turned his head so she would move her hand "There is *nothing* you can do to me to make me forget her."

"Maybe not," she stepped away from him, "but there may be a few things I can do to make her forget you."

"I will *kill* you!" He lunged forward. The chains clanked as she waved her hand to lift them up higher.

"Trust me, God of Frost. When it comes down to it, it will be *me* who kills *you*." She chuckled darkly. "And not shortly after I kill that insufferable trainee of yours."

Frost, I won't let her hurt you. I'm coming for you. I willed for him to hear me. Not even a few moments later, his head shot up in alert. He looked around the room as the Goddess of Fire took her exit and let the doors slam behind her.

"Wherever you are, Alli, do not do it." He muttered and shook his head. "You have no idea how dangerous they are."

I turned around, fearing nothing. I would not sit and let them torture him like they were. I exited through where I came in, seeing the Goddess of Light standing in the same spot.

"Alliana, I know you want to save him. There will be consequences for doing so. Consequences that nobody else is prepared for." She told me, putting her hand on my shoulder. "Go if you must, but it is not just his life you must be worried about."

I nodded and walked past her. I thought my breathing was shaky because of how angry I was, but in reality, my whole body was shaking. I looked down at my hands and realized how terrible it really was.

"Alli, what did you see?" Madisyn asked.

"If we're gonna save him, we have to go now." I could barely speak above a whisper. "There won't be another time to save him."

There was a look shared between Madisyn and Max before they both nodded firmly.

"We decided to help him when we came with you." Max offered. "We won't back out now just because there's a little danger. We're going."

I didn't know what I was getting them into. I could be dragging them down a path they couldn't return from. They knew that, of course, but were risking it all to help me – to help *Frost*.

I would never be able to repay them for what I was going to put them through.

CHAPTER ELEVEN

The room they held him in was very well hidden. They didn't want anyone to find him, especially us. If the Goddess of Light didn't let me see what was going on, I never would have known where to look.

Now, the door that the two Goddesses had walked through previously was sealed by brick. I closed my eyes as I tried to remember what the symbol was the Goddess of Light had drawn.

"Alli, what did you see?" Madisyn stopped me. "What were they doing to him?"

"The Goddess of Wind said they weren't going to kill him, but I think the Goddess of Fire wants to. They have him chained up in the middle of the room and all they do is go in there to taunt him." I told them as I started drawing the symbol on the bricks. The bricks slowly and quietly fell away, leaving the doors standing proudly behind.

I grabbed the handle and looked back and Max and Madisyn.

"Are you sure you want to do this?" I asked them with a concerned tone. "There's no turning back after you walk through these doors."

"We need to hurry, Alli. They might come back to watch him." Max said firmly. "We're not turning back."

I pushed the doors open and met Frost's eyes as soon as I walked through them. He opened his mouth to say something, but seeing Max and Madisyn with me changed his course of thought.

"You guys are going to get yourselves killed." He grumbled quietly. "I do not need saving."

"Says the guy in chains." I mocked him. "Shut up. We're getting you out of here." I grabbed his wrist carefully and he winced in pain.

"Alliana, I will be okay." He told me. "If you do this, there's no going back –"

"Exactly why I'm doing it." I cut him off. "There's no reason for them to do this to you. It's us against them now and I think we have a pretty good chance."

"You have no idea what you are doing, Alli." Frost looked from me to the other two trainees. "They will be in danger too."

"We accepted that when we agreed to help." Madisyn interjected as she grabbed his other wrist. "Now stop talking before they know someone's in here."

A look of shock appeared on his face as he nodded. "Well, there's no key. These are magically powered chains. They only respond to the Goddess of Fire."

"Yeah, we'll see about that." Maximo chuckled while holding his hand up to the ceiling. A slight rumble occurred and then the chains ripped from the ceiling along with a chunk of marble. "If we can't get them off, we'll just take them with us."

"She will be able to track them, Maximo." Frost replied. "You have maybe two minutes before she comes back. You should go now while you still can."

"Stop it." I whisper-shouted at him. "Do you understand that if you go down, we're going down with you? There is *no* way to talk us out of this, so shut up and take the damn help!"

"I...okay." Frost nodded slowly. "If you guys work together, you may have enough power to break them."

"I have an idea." I looked at Frost. "This might hurt...a little bit."

I grabbed his hands and ice coated the skin all the way up his arms.

"Can either of you use fire?" I asked them. Madisyn stepped forward.

"Are you sure about this?" She asked.

"Heat up the cuffs." I told her. "Max, get a rock ready."

The ceiling crumbled as Max broke a piece from it. The chains began to glow red and rapidly melt the ice. I squeezed his hands, sending as much power as I could to keep him covered in ice.

"Now, Max!" I looked at him. He slammed the rock down on the first cuff. We watched with smiles as it clattered to the floor in two pieces. He went to smash the other one. At the same time, we heard the brick wall behind the door crumbling.

"Quickly!" Frost's eyes widened in alarm.

The second cuff fell to the floor. He fell into me, unprepared to hold himself up. I looked at Madisyn and Max.

"Go, now!"

Max disappeared with a quick rumble and Madisyn gave me a look of worry before she, too, disappeared.

"Frost, I know you're weak right now, but I need a little bit of help." I lifted him to his feet.

I held onto him tightly and willed us away from the room with my powers. We were certainly running out of time. Just as I heard the doors open, we disappeared.

I'm sure the last thing the Goddess of Fire saw was a few shards of ice falling to the floor. We crash-landed onto the floor of my bedroom. Frost laid against the marble while breathing laboriously.

"We do not have a lot of time." Frost said, his eyes closed. "If we do not get out of here soon, they will close off the realm."

"Where am I supposed to take you if they do that?" I asked. "They'll find you in your realm."

"Yours, Alliana. We need to go to yours. They will not risk exposing the Power." He grunted as he sat up. "If we are going, we must go now!"

I grabbed onto him, and with every last bit of strength either of us had, we willed ourselves into the human realm. We must have fallen through the ceiling of my house. We landed hard on the dining room table and crushed it below us.

A scream sounded behind us as I looked to see my mother. She was a kind lady and she was the town doctor. She had long, straight, blonde hair and familiar, blue eyes that I thought I would never see again.

"Alliana?" She gasped.

"Mom, I know what it looks like, and it's a lot to explain, but he needs help. Now." I stood wobbly on my feet as I attempted to help him.

"What in the –?" Another familiar voice sounded from the doorway.

"Erin, we could use your help too." My mother stated. "We need to help him, quickly."

Erin was my best friend ever since I was little. She was the daughter of my mother's childhood best friend. She had bright, red hair and more freckles than stars in the sky. My mother and Erin quickly hoisted Frost up to his feet.

"You have a *lot* of explaining to do after this." Erin nodded towards me. I gave her a weak smile and a nod.

They set Frost up on the kitchen island. My mother started by checking his pulse.

"I don't even want to know who this is, Alli." My mother shook her head. "You leave for twenty minutes and you come back with a battered, bruised man and want us to fix him!"

"Twenty minutes?" I frowned.

"You left here not even an hour ago!" Erin confirmed.

I lifted my shaky hands and attempted to do something to help them. Frost opened his eyes, grabbing my arm.

"I will be okay." He muttered. "We need to get back as soon as possible."

"Oh, no." My mother said. "You aren't going anywhere until I fix you up. When's the last time you ate?"

Erin pulled me into the other room with an angry look on her face.

"Who the hell is that?" She whisper-yelled at me. "Do you know how crazy this is? Where did you even meet this guy? What's his name?"

"Erin, I promise you I will explain everything, but I need to know he'll be alright." I said as my voice began to shake. Her angry look turned into one of sympathy.

"How long have you been seeing him?" She asked. "Where did you even meet him? I've never seen him before in my life. You know, you're right. Let's go make sure he's okay."

After a while, they decided Frost needed to rest. They did as much as they could for him and then put him on the couch. I helped my mother and Erin pick up the demolished table.

"You have quite a bit of explaining to do, young lady." My mother said as she folded her arms.

To explain everything was much harder than I thought it would be. I told them about the first encounter with Frost when I was eight, and again when I saw him in the field last. I explained to them the challenges, the things that happened to me during them, and how I ended up falling for my mentor, the God of Frost, along the way.

I told them how he looked out for me and helped me even when he knew he wasn't supposed to. I told them how I slowly broke down his walls and got him to trust me. There were so many things I had to tell them in such little time.

All they needed to know was that I needed Frost. I needed him to be happy and healthy, but most of all, I needed him to be himself. I explained how I hoped, although I knew it would never happen, that Frost and I could just stay here and avoid the rest of the Gods all together.

They were amazed at the trials I went through and astonished that I made it. They knew Frost had to be something special if I had my eyes on him (or so my mother said).

They sat there in awe as I explained in vivid detail the things I'd seen. From the other trainees risking everything to help me out to the challenge where Max and Derek got into a fight.

We were all human – imperfectly human – and that is what made us so great.

Without even realizing it, I allowed Maximo and Madisyn to get into a pit of insanity. They were willing to risk everything because of my feelings for Frost. I was right to trust them, but I was wrong to leave them there alone.

What if the Goddess of Fire knew they helped me? She must know that there was no way I would be able to get him out of there myself. I began to sweat. I knew I had to go back eventually. I was getting nervous.

What if I led Max and Madisyn to their deaths unintentionally?

"Alli...that sounds incredibly wild." Erin shook her head with her mouth slightly ajar. "I swear, you haven't even been gone more than an hour. Is time different there?"

"I guess it must be." I looked at my feet, leaning against the counter. "If I end up leaving, you have to keep him here. The second he goes to that realm, they'll kill him."

"If he has powers like you say he does, we won't be able to keep him here if that's what he wants." My mother said with an empathetic look in her eye. "I'm sure he'll want to help you if you do go. You're probably in just as much danger."

"But I didn't break the rules, Mom, he did. And he broke out of his punishment." I shook my head. "He can't go back. He's the biggest target there."

"Honey, he's a grown man. He'll be able to fend for himself. I'm sure he has before. Besides, they won't kill him in front of everyone. That's awfully cruel." My mother offered.

"I don't know, Ma. They're pretty horrific." I told her. "The things they've said and done to him already..."

"I'm still confused." Erin rattled her head. "So, you can fall in love with some major God, but not with the friendly neighbor boy who's been in love with you for ten years?"

"Erin, not funny." I chuckled and rolled my eyes. She gave me a beaming smile to tell me she was messing with me.

We sat in the kitchen and discussed what I was going to do. I knew I had to go back soon, but it was going to be hard to keep Frost here if I left. He would want to go after me as I went after him.

I languished as I ran my fingers through my hair. I looked

at Frost sleeping peacefully on my mother's couch. There was something so surreal about this. Why couldn't things just be normal? Why did our relationship have to be against the rules?

You can play fair with someone you love, just as easy as you could with anyone else.

Whatever the outcome of this was, I knew it was going to take a lot of work in order to fix everything. The Goddess of Fire, clearly, was very angry. I'm sure she was wreaking havoc on everyone and anyone even partly responsible for watching Frost.

I worried for the Goddess of Light, who had so reluctantly given up Frost's location. She knew Frost was in danger and wanted to protect him as much as I did. The Goddess of Light, much like Madisyn and Max, would do anything for her friends. She put herself on the line because she knew exactly what made Frost happy.

Suddenly, the house began to shake. The three of us quickly stood alert. I watched as the lights flickered and immediately Frost shot up from the couch. He looked over at us. His eyes were the most radiant blue I had ever seen.

"The War has begun. Destroy all to become one."

CHAPTER TWELVE

"Frost?" I ran over to his side as he rocked back and forth while reciting the same line. "Frost!" As soon as I touched him, his eyes faded back to their normal shade of blue.

"Alliana, we have to go." He uttered quietly. "Somebody has died and the war has begun."

"The war?" I questioned. "No, Frost, you need to rest."

"You do not understand!" He stood briskly. "Everybody you love will *die* if we do not go now!"

"Frost, what are you talking about?" I snatched his bicep to keep him from walking away.

"The war was the end goal the whole time, Alliana. That is why the Gods take on trainees, so the war can take place. The Gods train their successors to the best of their ability and then they fight to the death. The only way for me to know it started is if the first kill happened." He rambled quickly. "You understand why I could not tell you before, right?"

"That doesn't matter right now, Frost." I told him with a face of disbelief. "I'm sure there's more to it, but if the war *has* started, you need to stay here."

"What? No way am I staying here, Alli. The trainees are nowhere near strong enough to take us on yet. Everyone will *die* if we do not-"

"*I'll* go, but you're staying." I said firmly. "My mother will take care of you. The only way to keep you safe is for you to stay here. This isn't about me or the other trainees. We did this to rescue *you*. If we die trying, we die trying. End of story. Stay here."

I turned towards my mother and Erin and gave them the gravest stare I could.

"Do *not* let him leave. His life depends on it."

He said for him to know if the war started, someone must've died.

Who died?

✳ ✳ ✳ ✳ ✳ ✳ ✳

MADISYN'S POV: THE BEGINNING OF THE WAR

After Alliana left, Max and I made it back to our rooms. Within minutes of settling down, the Goddess of Fire called everyone to a meeting. It was very obvious that Alliana and the God of Frost were missing.

The God of Frost's usual chair sat empty on the right next to the Goddess of Light's. I made eye contact with her. She had an unusual tint in her eyes.

"There are *traitors* among us." The Goddess of Fire spat violently. "The God of Frost and his trainee, Alliana, had the worst intentions for all of you. We detained the God of Frost in an attempt to hinder their plans."

"That's such a lie." Derek scoffed quietly in my ear. "She's *evil*."

"You're just now figuring that out?" I furrowed my eyebrows at him. "You gotta try better than that."

"With all of you here, I would like to let everyone know exactly who the traitor is." The Goddess of Fire's eyes scanned the room. "This traitor will be put to death, as will the God of Frost and Alliana once we find them."

Fear coursed through my veins as I watched her survey the crowd. Did she know Max and I helped Alliana save Frost? I mean, I was glad they got out, but there was that underlying feeling of regret.

The Goddess of Fire became surrounded by a large flame as her gaze turned upon the other Gods. My blood ran cold as she found her target – the Goddess of Light.

"You are...despicable."

She didn't even give the Goddess of Light time to say anything.

One fireball from her palm and the Goddess of Light was engulfed in flames. Her blood-curdling screams could be heard from the other side of the colosseum.

I turned away quickly. I was unable to watch as the Goddess of Fire turned back towards the trainees. She gave off an evil laugh as she sent a fireball to the ceiling.

"Welcome to the war." She said calmly as the doors flew open behind us. "Run...or die."

❋ ❋ ❋ ❋ ❋ ❋ ❋

ALLIANA'S POV

As soon as I entered the realm again, I found myself in an empty courtyard. The buildings around me were on fire and it looked like an absolute warzone. I scanned around quickly in an attempt to find someone.

I studied the sky in awe as I saw two of the Gods fighting overhead. This, I assumed, was the most divided War the Gods and Goddesses had ever seen. I hastily walked into one of the buildings.

I was met with the God of Water. I stopped and drew back.

"She killed her because of you." The God of Water clicked his tongue. "She was...extraordinary. She trusted you and now she is dead." She killed *who*? A tidal wave of water began to form behind him.

At this point, I didn't even feel scared. I had a mission to free my friends and to get Frost back here safely.

"Who? Who died?"

"As if you don't know." He huffed.

"I *don't*. I found Frost chained up in a colosseum so I rescued him. They were *torturing* him. You know damn well Frost has always been good." I babbled quickly. "You also know just as well as I do everything the Goddess of Fire told you is a lie. She and the Goddess of Wind were torturing him."

The wave behind him slowly dissipated as he listened to my words. He gave a long sigh. I knew I wouldn't be able to defeat him on my own, so I was trying my best to get him on my side.

"The Goddess of Fire killed the Goddess of Light. I do not know where the other trainees are, but I know your friends are safe...for now." He stepped to the side to move out of my way. "I wish you well. And the God of Frost, too. He always did have the best intentions."

"Thank you." I nodded as I ran past him. "I won't forget this."

I turned down the closest corridor, racing towards the unknown. There was no guarantee the next God or Goddess I ran into would be my ally.

As I ran past a door, it swung open. Someone grabbed my arm and yanked me into it. A slight yelp came from my lips as the doors closed again.

I was in a closet. There were shelves upon shelves of random items and memorabilia. Maximo, Madisyn, and Derek were all sitting on the ground and staring at me expectantly.

"You couldn't have just told me to come in here?" I let out a breath of repose. "I got stopped by the God of Water on my way over here. I was scared to figure out who was next."

"The Goddess of Fire killed –"

"The Goddess of Light, I know." I bobbed my head. "What the hell even happened?"

"The Goddess of Fire called you and Frost traitors. We were so scared she was going to point us out as your accomplices, but she thought it was the Goddess of Light." Maximo explained quietly. "Next thing you know, the whole building's on fire and she tells us if we all don't run, we'll all die next."

"I think she said something about a war?" Derek added. "I can't believe I used to think she was cool. Now she's trying to kill us!"

"Frost told me the war was essentially a battle between the old and the new. We're supposed to fight the Gods to the death, like survival of the fittest. I guess it usually starts after there's been more training." I explained to them. "Frost and I probably set it off early."

"But...a few of the trainees are still working with their

mentors..." Madisyn looked sullen. "They think it's just the Goddess of Fire against them. Are they still in danger?"

"They must be." I confirmed her doubts. "The Goddess of Light was the only other one I knew we could trust. The Goddess of Wind is certainly against us."

"I think the God of Healing would be on our side." Madisyn said. "There's no way he would be okay with senseless killing."

"There's no way to be sure. There's us and that's it. Don't trust anybody with your life if they are not in this room." I instructed them. "We should stick together, but we need to keep moving."

"Where are we going to go?" Derek asked. "We're in danger everywhere!"

"There's only one way to win this war, Derek." I looked at each one of them. "We have to start taking these guys out."

❋ ❋ ❋ ❋ ❋ ❋ ❋

We ran across the open courtyard. At one point, it was full of beautiful green hedges. Now, it looked like a bomb went off. Everything was on fire. The Goddess of Fire apparently took quite a toll on this realm.

"Do we really have to kill them?" Madisyn asked. "That seems against everything the God of Healing has ever taught me."

"That's the only way they won't kill you, Madisyn." I replied. "It's going to be hard, but it's us or them."

"Yeah, Mads, they've been alive a few centuries. We need a turn." Max cracked a quick smile at the two of us. "Too soon?"

"The second they all know I'm back, it's game on." I said. "I'll be their first target."

As if on command, a small tornado swept through the clearing. It quickly faded away and the Goddess of Wind stepped out of it. I walked in front of the other trainees. I was willing to risk myself to save them.

I couldn't remember a time before my training I was *ever* willing to risk myself. Maybe I never *was* willing. Now, there was something worth fighting for and worth losing *everything* over.

"Well, well, well..." The Goddess of Wind smirked at me. "I

should have known the four of you would cause trouble." The wind around us was becoming almost strong enough to knock me over.

"You've caused all the trouble." I growled at her. I felt the power surging through me as I watched her closely.

"Oh, dear. The God of Frost really made you think you were a match for *me*?" She laughed condescendingly. "There is one difference between the God of Frost and I. One...significant difference giving me the advantage."

"What would that be?" I asked. Madisyn brushed against my shoulder as she prepared to fight alongside me.

"I am not in love with you. You, as one being, are not enough to defeat me." She took a step closer to me. "And here you are...all alone."

"Who said she was alone?" Madisyn's voice was stern.

"She's got more people behind her than you ever have." Max matched Madisyn's tone. Derek walked up to join Max as well.

"Quality has always meant more than quantity, children." The Goddess of Wind chuckled. "Even your combined strengths are not enough to defeat me."

"Frost was right." I taunted. "You are pathetic."

Her anger was visible on her face as it wrinkled into something horrible. Her hair began whipping around her as the wind picked up. Soon enough, it was so bad I could barely hear what anyone was saying.

"Alliana! Look!" Madisyn's frantic voice caught my attention as I followed her eyes. A tornado, a huge one, was barreling toward us at a lively speed.

"We have to jump in!" I yelled at them.

"Jump in? Are you nuts? That thing'll tear us apart!" Maximo's eyes were wide.

"If we can get inside the tornado, we can disrupt its course. We just have to make it hot and change the wind current. I can't do that alone!" Before I even realized what was happening, Derek grabbed my arm.

"I think I'm the best contender for this one." His eyes were full of determination.

"You guys might want to stand back." I told Madisyn and Max. "If we don't make it...find Frost for me, please."

Derek and I shared one more look before we ran towards the tornado. The wind was strong and nearly pulled us off our feet.

I looked back once more at Maximo and Madisyn, who attempted to distract the Goddess of Wind with their powers.

"You alright?" Derek shouted.

"Never been better."

Together, we leapt into the tornado.

CHAPTER THIRTEEN

The wind whipped us around. I was barely able to gain my composure, but I made eye contact with Derek. As soon as I did, his eyes began to glow a bright red. I closed my own eyes while feeling the power struggle to flow through me.

I willed it as best as I could as I clenched my fists. I felt heat hovering around me, and when I opened my eyes I saw streaks of flames running through the tornado. With a loud scream, I released every bit of power I could.

The feeling of the power rolling through me was unlike anything I ever felt before. I felt strong, but I was slowly being drained as I drew more and more power into me. I could feel the blood running through my veins and I could hear my heart pumping deep within my ears.

The raging wind was met with another gust going in the opposite direction. The tornado began to dissipate quickly, leaving Derek and I falling through the air. Derek's eyes changed back to his normal color. They were wide with fear as we plummeted towards the ground. I closed my eyes as I braced for impact.

Suddenly, I landed on something soft. I opened my eyes slowly and saw a chunk of earth below us. Maximo led Derek and I steadily to the ground before the mounds crumbled below us.

The Goddess of Wind was gone.

"Where did she go?"

"Not sure, but what I am sure of...is you guys just kicked her ass." Maximo smiled widely. "That was absolutely amazing."

"We would've been squashed on the ground if it weren't for

you. You two distracted her well." Derek chuckled. "That was pretty cool for all of us."

"Where did you get the idea to jump into the tornado?" Madisyn asked me.

"That was my challenge. Her idea for my challenge was to have me jump into a tornado. It was…an experience." I explained to them. "We should keep moving, though. We don't know who we're going to encounter next."

We made our way across the open clearing. We entered the first set of doors we saw and found the colosseum empty for our use. The emblems on the chairs belonging to the Gods were all glowing, except two: the Goddess of Light and Frost's. The Goddess of Wind's was a bit dimmer than the rest but still glowed proudly.

Before, there was no acknowledgment of the trainees. Now, where the Gods' portraits once stood, were portraits of us. The emblems on the frames glowed as brightly as the ones upon the Gods' chairs.

"They're keeping score." Madisyn muttered with her voice shaky. "They know who's alive."

"But they're wrong." I interjected. "Frost just isn't in this realm. He is very much alive."

"Do you think…do you think he's killed people before?" She asked me.

"I don't know." I shook my head. "I'd like to believe he didn't, but if that's why he's alive…then so be it."

The colosseum began to shake violently as one of the lights for the trainees went out. We all turned and watched as the emblem on Lance's portrait faded into nothing.

"Oh, God." Madisyn covered her mouth with her palm and looked away.

Soon after that, the doors behind us swung open. The Goddess of Darkness and the God of Healing came storming into the room. They took one look at us and then at the seats behind them.

"Board up the doors." The God of Healing looked at the

Goddess of Darkness. "Nobody in, nobody out." His voice was darker than it usually was. As soon as the words left his mouth, the Goddess of Darkness began sealing the door.

The four of us began to slowly back into the corner. We had no idea what to expect. We didn't know who was friend or foe anymore. Madisyn and I made eye contact. She had the same worried gleam in her eye that I was sure I had.

"You have no idea what you have done." The God of Healing looked at me. "By saving the God of Frost, you have catapulted your fellow trainees into something they have not yet been trained for. Any lives lost are on *your* hands."

"She wasn't alone." Madisyn intervened. "It's on all of us. None of us knew the consequence, but we knew there would be one. We weren't going to sit here and let them kill Frost."

"Then you are more foolish than I thought." The God of Healing was still completely calm. "Despite that, what you have done is brave. May you always live with this decision." He bowed slightly at me.

"It was a decision I would make a thousand times over." I told him, beginning to relax.

"One day...one day you may change your mind." The Goddess of Darkness said. "We already lost the Goddess of Light. She has been my partner for...millennia. It got to the point I was sure nothing would ever overtake us." She looked at her feet with an evident sadness overtaking her features.

"She wanted me to help Frost." My heart sunk at the thought of the Goddess of Darkness losing her best friend.

"I know." The Goddess of Darkness gave a small smile. "She and the God of Frost have been friends longer than I have known her. The last thing you must think is that she regrets helping him. Their bond is...different. They will find each other again."

I sighed and hoped that she wouldn't be able to tell I was riddled with a sour feeling. Frost had been alive all these years – longer than written history – and he, somehow, never once mentioned his past. Did he and the Goddess of Light have something *more*?

"With that being said...I have never seen the God of Frost act the way he does now, because of you. He is...less of the coldhearted, distant man he usually is." She reached over and touched my shoulder. "He, for lack of a better term, is cold. He has no idea how to be anything else. I believe you are making him feel something for the first time in a long, long time. That is another reason the Goddess of Light sacrificed herself. She knows what bond you and the God of Frost have."

I affirmed and looked away from her. I wasn't sure what else to say or how to respond to that. The Goddess of Light died unnecessarily. She put herself on the line to save an old friend. That wasn't something most could say they would do.

"Enough." The God of Healing intervened. "We need to come up with a plan. There are things that are yet to happen that will test everyone's loyalties. I assume you know where the God of Frost is, Alliana?"

"Of course I know where he is." I sulked. "And I won't tell you."

"I am not asking you to tell me. I am just making sure he is safe."

"He's safe where he's at. Nobody will find him. His power has been masked." I expressed to him. "We should keep moving, though. If we stay here too long, somebody will find us."

"We are ready for whoever is coming, Alliana." The Goddess of Darkness said. "There is nothing to fear."

"I'm sure that's what the Goddess of Light thought too." I urged her. "The Goddess of Fire is too strong for us."

"Believe me when I tell you there is nothing stronger than the wrath of an angry God." The Goddess of Darkness said as her eyes faded black. "She may put up a fight, but she is no match for me." A chill ran down my spine as her eyes flickered back to normal.

"I still say we need to move." Madisyn encouraged everyone. "I don't feel comfortable sitting here and waiting for someone to find us."

"No. You will stay here." The God of Healing replied.

"You can't *make* us sit here." Derek interjected. "Aren't we supposed to be fighting each other anyway?"

The ground beneath us rumbled heavily. A few parts of the ceiling shattered against the floor. We all looked around while waiting for somebody to burst through the walls or the door.

My head snapped over to the Gods' emblems. The God of Water's emblem shone brightly before going out altogether.

"No!" Max festered as he looked at the God of Healing. "Let us out. I have to find him!"

"He is *dead*, Maximo!" The Goddess of Darkness cried out. "He is dead. There is no longer anything you can do. You are safe here, with all of us."

Another lustrous light flashed as Lindsay's portrait faded to black. Madisyn grabbed my arm while fear contorted her face.

"You can't honestly expect us to stay here while people are *dying* out there." I pointed to the portraits. "These are our friends."

"I sat and watched the Goddess of Light die – we *all* did. The only way you will make it through this is if we stick together." The Goddess of Darkness said.

"That's not true and you know it." Derek scoffed. "The four of us could outpower any one of you Gods. You don't scare us."

"Derek..."

"You think you're big and bad, but you probably haven't ever lifted a finger in a situation like this! You let the other Gods do your dirty work!"

The lights went out.

The four of us backed up so our shoulders touched as we prepared to make defensive moves. Maximo sighed angrily.

"You had to work her up, didn't you?" He asked grumpily.

"Hey, don't blame me for this whole situation. They walked in here after we did. I say winner takes all." Derek shrugged, his voice sharp.

"We walked in here as four and we're leaving as four." I replied to them as strongly as I could. "Nobody gets left behind."

The doors slammed open. A familiar grumbling sound grew closer and closer to us. I squeezed my fists, shut my eyes, and willed every bit of my power out. As I opened my eyes, I lifted my hand towards the ceiling. A beam of light shot from my palm into the top of the curved ceiling. The light drifted down the wooden beams and lit up the colosseum around us.

The Goddess of Darkness laid her back against the ceiling and effortlessly clung to it. Her eyes were completely dark as she watched our every move. One of the creatures from the maze was crawling around her in a circle.

"You must pick and choose your battles wisely, children." Her voice became hoarse. It made the hair on the back of my neck stand straight.

"Great! Now we have a psycho demon chick against us. Thanks, Derek." Max grumbled under his breath.

"I think we can take her." I shrugged. "Stick together. She can't kill all of us." I gripped Madisyn's arm.

Without warning, a loud shriek erupted from the creature as it dove onto the floor. Its eyes were entirely white and it was obviously blind. I took slow, quiet breaths as I gradually backed closer into my circle.

The Goddess of Darkness's hair was wriggling around the ceiling like a ton of tiny snakes. The ground began to reverberate.

"I've had enough." Max bellowed. He forced the ground beneath the creature to crack open and swallow it. He then closed it, broke off a pillar, and sent it flying towards the Goddess of Darkness.

Derek quickly joined him and sent a shot of fire up to join the pillar. Before the Goddess of Darkness could process what was happening, she was pinned to the ceiling. The fire encircled her as she attempted to push the pillar away.

"We shouldn't kill her." Madisyn exclaimed. "We can't turn into them. Killing them will make us just as bad."

"We kill her or she kills us." I replied. Derek glanced at me.

"I don't know, Alli." Derek hesitated. "I don't like this idea."

"If you won't do it, I will." I snapped. I lifted my hand in haste. A gust of wind blew across the room, sending the circle of fire into the Goddess of Darkness. Her whole body ignited in flames as her screams tore through the room.

"Alli!" Max grabbed my arm and pulled me into him. The pillar that was once holding her up was seconds away from crashing into the floor. As soon as it did, we looked over at the Gods' chairs. The Goddess of Darkness's emblem exploded in light and then withered to blackness.

Her body, unlike the pillar, was still stuck to the ceiling. The torches lit once again one by one. A dark cloud escaped from the Goddess' mouth. It drifted down and it floated in front of me. The other trainees stood behind me. We all shared an incredulous look.

I shrank away from it, unsure of what to do. I wasn't sure what was happening. A flash of lightning could be seen from the window and shortly after we heard a crack of thunder. I started shaking as I turned back to see the sinister cloud.

"Alliana, what's happening?" Max asked quietly.

"I...I don't know." I whispered. I felt one of them grab onto my arm.

Before I knew it, the cloud quickly moved forward until it collided with me. I gasped as I felt a strange, airy feeling inside of me. There was a surge of energy whirling through me. It felt similar to a sugar rush; I was shaking and I felt lightheaded.

There was a burning sensation on my wrist. I griped loudly in pain as I looked down to see what was happening. The Goddess of Darkness's emblem was being seared into the skin on my wrist. I watched in horror as it completed.

The emblem on my portrait split in two. Half was Frost's and half was the Goddess of Darkness's.

"What just happened?" Madisyn asked breathlessly. I gulped.

"I think you're looking at the next Goddess of Darkness."

CHAPTER FOURTEEN

"How is that even possible?" Derek frowned.

"She killed her. She became the next Goddess." Maximo explained. "That must be the goal here. This war, or whatever it is, must be something like survival of the fittest. The strongest come out on top and the weakest don't make it."

"But she wasn't my mentor. I don't know how I would get her powers." I scowled and stared at the newly branded mark on my arm. "She's been alive so long. How was it so easy for us to kill her?"

"They must not be completely immortal." Derek proposed. "They might just not age. I mean, look how easily the Goddess of Fire killed the Goddess of Light."

"This is...insane." Max remarked. "So, if we kill a God, we *become* that God?"

"Don't be ridiculous. They all only have one power. If that were the case, then each God could have multiple powers." Madisyn explained.

"Well, *maybe* they're all just killers."

"Can you all *please* stop?" I snapped while whipping around to face them. "This isn't the time to discuss that! All of the remaining Gods know she's been killed and it's only a matter of time before they come here. We have to go *now*."

I turned and walked towards the doors. The others trailed behind me. I shuttered as worry sank deep inside me. I didn't understand what my new power even was. I wasn't familiar with the extent of it. The uncertainty made me sweat.

"Alli, are you okay?" Max asked, grabbing my arm as Madisyn and Derek continued down the hallway.

"I don't know." I tottered. "I feel lightheaded and shaky. Her power is too strong for me."

"You're wrong." Max replied, furrowing his eyebrows. "You're stronger than all of us, actually. We would have died if you didn't make the decision earlier. We would have died a *lot* of times if it weren't for you. Don't think like that. You're stronger than all of the Gods and us."

❊ ❊ ❊ ❊ ❊ ❊ ❊

We caught up with Madisyn and Derek at the end of the hallway. We exited out of the building. The rain was pouring down like tiny bullets and soaked us almost immediately. Despite how hard the rain was coming down, fires still raged at the buildings in the distance.

The once beautiful land that we frequented turned desolate, a warzone. The windows of nearly every building were shattered. There were craters in the ground from powerful attacks unleashed on enemies and friends.

It was devastating to watch as different areas of the realm were torn to pieces. I had always seen it as a glorious, untouchable place. I was wrong. The longer I sat there and thought about the war and all of the aspects that went into it, I grew increasingly concerned.

Frost didn't once mention anything about any wars. He never told me there would be a danger that could potentially cost my friends and I our lives. He never said that one day, we would all turn into stone-cold killers.

Yes, the Goddess of Darkness attacked us first. She definitely would have killed all of us if we let her escape. I looked back at the other three trainees and a warm feeling settled into my heart. These three people were going to extraordinary lengths to protect others they had just met.

Certain things happen for a reason. Other things happen just to happen. I met Frost for a reason, and I met Madisyn, Derek, and

Max for a reason as well. Albeit, they were different reasons, but reasons nonetheless.

I looked at the three of them, unsure of what to do. I put them through so much danger without thinking twice. I would never be able to repay any of them for the things they did for me.

"Alli, it's gonna be okay." Madisyn said quietly as we made our way across the plot of land. We had to climb over rubble from buildings that had since collapsed.

"It's not me I'm worried about." I glanced at Max.

"What do you mean?" She pouted as she stopped atop a pillar base.

"He said some things earlier. I don't think he expects to make it out of this." I shrugged. I continued on, leaving her stagnant. The boys were a bit in front of us having a conversation of their own.

"Do any of us really think we'll make it out?" Madisyn replied.

"I had a small hope." I cracked a gentle smile. "I guess it's not really about that though, is it?"

"No, I guess not."

We reached the building on the other side of the clearing. Just before we entered, the rain stopped. We paused and looked around. My clothes stuck uncomfortably to my skin as the chill from the rain quickly disappeared from the air.

"I have been waiting for you, dear Alliana." The Goddess of Fire's voice echoed through the area. "Now, you are mine."

"Run!" Max shouted.

Madisyn and Derek turned and ran into the building, but I was frozen to my spot. This was the moment I'd been waiting for. I knew she would find me at one point.

"Alli, now!" Max yanked on my arm, forcing me to follow him inside the building.

"I'm who she wants, Max, you guys can still make it out of here!" I told him as we ran down the hall after Derek and Madisyn.

"All of us know you have to make it out of here. You're the only one who knows where Frost is now." He replied. We ended up in a room with tall shelves filled with books. The books looked ancient like they were just as old as the Gods themselves.

"Board up the doors, guys. She's coming." I told them urgently. The four of us quickly got to work, pushing anything and everything we could in front of the doors.

"Try to seal the doors with the Goddess of Darkness's power." Derek suggested. "She was able to do it."

"I've never done that before, Derek. I don't know how." I replied, shrugging. "I don't know how to trigger her power either, only Frost's."

"This won't be enough to hold her off, Alli. You have to try." Madisyn encouraged. "I'm sure it'll come naturally for you."

A strange feeling of ambiguity overcame me as I looked at the double doors in front of us. I thought about it. What gave the Goddess of Darkness her Power? For Frost, it was easy. I could just think about it and it would happen.

I closed my eyes and attempted to put myself in complete darkness. I walked over to the hinges of the door on the right and gently touched it with the tips of my fingers. I ran my fingers along the trim, slowly opening my eyes.

Nothing.

I let go of a breath I didn't even realize I was holding. I turned to look at the other trainees, and as I did, the ground shook around us. There was a bang on the door that sent a couple of the objects against it flying.

I winced and quickly stepping back to be with the others. I could feel it all over again. We were tensing up for a battle. The only difference this time was the uncertainty of taking on the Goddess of Fire.

She, for a lack of a better term, was certainly fiery. She had an attitude one hundred percent of the time and, quite frankly, didn't give a damn about anyone if they were in her way. She stomped down the competition, just like she was about to stomp us down.

We finally met our match.

I remembered the blind creatures the Goddess of Darkness summoned shortly before her death. Did that mean I could now summon them too? Could I use them to protect us, even for a short moment?

I clenched my eyes shut and willed all of the power to me I could. I felt stronger with the power of darkness swirling inside me. It was an evil feeling I felt as I called for the same creatures that once terrified us.

Another bang on the door ensued as I opened my eyes. I saw three of the creatures crawling on the ceiling. Without saying anything, they knew exactly what I wanted. As soon as she came in the door, they were on strict orders to kill.

"Did you...?"

"Yes."

I looked over at Max. There was a gleam in his eye. It was a sort of mischievous gleam, but I knew he had the best intentions. The objects against the door clattered against the floor as she got closer and closer to entering the room.

"Is now a bad time for the 'all for one and one for all' speech?" Max asked with a nervous chuckle. "Because that's about all I got for encouragement."

"Never needed it more than I do right now." Derek muttered in reassurance while nudging Max slightly.

The creatures I summoned were still on the apex of the ceiling and crawling around restlessly as they awaited their target. I knew with just one more hit on the door, the Goddess of Fire would be upon us. There was no way she was going to let us escape.

The doors burst open. The Goddess of Fire charged in with the brightest red eyes. We collectively took a step back.

"Get down!" I screamed. I attempted to pull them down with me as a ring of fire spread across the room.

"You *fools* think you can defeat me?" She cackled evilly and threw her head back. She shot a ball of fire from her hand that caught a bookshelf behind us. "Stand up and fight, then."

One of the creatures sprung from the ceiling with a shriek and landed directly on her back. As soon as it touched her, it disintegrated into ashes. I covered my mouth with my hand to suppress my gasp. This woman was literally untouchable.

"The Goddess of Darkness was pathetic anyway, Alliana." She tilted her head to the side and mocked a sympathetic look. "How... *fitting* you have received her powers."

Another fireball came straight for us. It crushed the ground where we once stood as we leapt back.

We scrambled in different directions. We made our way behind various objects as fire flew around recklessly.

I caught Max's eyes. He was determined. He was going to help us any way he could. I swallowed hard remembering the conversation we had earlier.

"You're wrong." Max replied, furrowing his eyebrows. "You're stronger than all of us, actually. We would have died if you didn't make the decision earlier. We would have died a lot of times if it weren't for you. Don't think like that. You're stronger than all of the Gods and us."

"You know that's not true." I scoffed, shaking my head.

"Alliana, I want you to know that all of us – and I mean all *of us - are prepared to die for this battle. We're not just doing this for you or Frost anymore. At least I know for me that I need to prove myself." Max put his hands in his pockets. He avoided direct eye contact as he formulated his words. "I need to prove to myself that all of this is for a reason. I need to know there is a greater good and that greater good is you. You need to fix this terrible world and everything in it."*

"Max, what are you..."

"I'm not done, Alli. We don't have a lot of time." He interrupted me. "Just know every decision we make is independent of you. The blood the Goddess of Darkness said was on your hands is not on your hands at all. No matter what happens to me, or to anyone, you can't blame yourself, okay? If I do something, it's for a reason. Believe that and accept it."

At that exact moment, I figured out what he wanted from me. He knew he was going to die. He just wanted to do it with honor.

All for one and one for all.

"Max, don't." I begged. "You won't make it."

"What are you talking about?" Madisyn's eyes dilated. Objects crashed around us and burned to ashes right in front of us.

"If you don't leave, we'll all die. You guys have to go." Max said with a stern look in his eye. "Alliana, please."

I breathed heavily for a moment as I processed his request. My heart broke in two as I saw the desperate look on his face. It wasn't me he wanted to save anymore. Hell, he didn't even want to save himself at this point.

"Derek, Madisyn, let's go." I told them hesitantly.

"You can't actually want us to leave Max..." Madisyn said.

"It's not what I want anymore." I snapped. "*Now.*"

A fireball whizzed past our heads and smashed the window in front of us. That was our opportunity.

"You have no idea who you are dealing with." The Goddess of Fire's voice echoed throughout the room as the three of us crawled towards the window. Derek and Madisyn climbed out first. I hesitated and turned back to look at Max.

He gave me one strong nod before I left out the window.

CHAPTER FIFTEEN

We crossed back over the clearing but this time we were one short. Everyone was silent as we quickly attempted to get out of the open area. I held back tears as I thought about the battle Max was fighting – not only physically, but mentally.

I didn't have a clue why he wanted to sacrifice himself for us, but I did my best to obey his wishes. He did so much for me in such a little amount of time. I couldn't even fathom how to begin repaying him.

In the end, all he wanted was to put himself on the line for the rest of us. He was valiant and brave; there was no doubt in my mind he would fight until he couldn't anymore.

"You know what?" Madisyn snapped. "Forget this! I can't sit here and let this happen. Are you serious right now? After everything he's done for you, you're just going to let him die?"

"Madisyn, hold on..."

"No, I don't *care*. You're going to let an innocent man – I'm sorry, *another* innocent man – die because you have some fantasy with Frost?" She continued on. "There's no reason to turn your back on Max when we could *beat* her together!"

I raised my hand and pinned her against an upright pillar with a block of ice. "For one, we couldn't have beaten her. Not right now. We're too weak and she's too strong. Second, I would *never* leave Max behind if he hadn't asked me to."

"He did what?" Derek's was surprised as his attention directed to me.

"I don't know why, but he said he needed to prove himself." I spelled out for them. "And I understand it's hard. I feel the same pain you do. So, compose yourselves. We still have a war to win." My hand dropped to my side and the ice surrounding Madisyn dissolved to the ground.

"You're turning into him, you know." Madisyn's eyes watered. *"Cold-hearted."*

I chose to ignore her as we made our way back to the colosseum. I was curious about the updates. I wanted to see who else was dead and who was alive. The further away we got from the Goddess of Fire the better.

We entered in the doors hesitantly. My soul was afflicted seeing the familiar rubble from this warzone still scattered along the floor. A few more of the Gods' emblems faded to nothing. Only the Goddess of Fire, the Goddess of Wind, the God of Earth, and the God of Healing remained. There seemed to be an extra glow coming from their seats. I heard a sniffle come from Madisyn.

We looked at the trainees' portraits and I choked back my own tears. Max's portrait was beginning to fade. Madisyn started sobbing as she fell to the floor. I could tell Derek's eyes were beginning to water as well, despite his best efforts to hide it.

I couldn't look at Madisyn as she sobbed. It ravaged my heart thinking that I caused all of this. I caused all of it...and for what? For *Frost*?

My opinion about Frost was so dependent on everything I'd learned in the past few weeks. Frost was a great mentor; he was the best teacher I could've asked for. He was...strange in the way he couldn't *tell* me he felt something for me.

In fact, I don't even think he knew it was possible. My heart and mind both craved to see him. I wanted to make sure he was okay, and that my mother was able to keep him in our realm.

"After we win this, we won't be like them." Derek declared. "I won't put anyone through this."

"Agreed." I nodded with my throat incredibly dry.

All that was left of us trainees were the three of us in the room, Apolonia, and Victoria. I wasn't even aware of the tears streaming down my face until I wiped my cheek. I took a deep, shaky breath. We only had moments before the Goddess of Fire was upon us again and this time we would have no choice but to fight.

I sat beside Madisyn on the ground and wrapped my arm around her shoulder. Unfortunately, the power of healing could only heal physical wounds, not mental ones.

"I don't blame you." She whispered through her tears. "I'm sorry." She began to wipe them away.

"It's okay, Mads." I gave her a reassuring smile. "We're all on edge right now. We'll figure this out. We'll avenge his death."

"Good." She nodded. "Let's make sure he didn't die for nothing, yeah?"

I stood and lent her my hand. Her face was red and puffy as she got back up to her feet. The anchoring sadness within us grew but there would be time to grieve after the Gods were defeated.

The ground vibrated around us once more. There was a sense of uneasiness in the room. We were all beginning to doubt our abilities, despite making it this far.

The whole concept of this *war* was so wrong. We were trained by the Gods to kill the Gods. Winner takes all. Kill a God and obtain their power. It was ridiculous! The Gods knew they were stronger than us and knew they would win.

But not this time! This time, I refused to be another play in their book of a millennia's worth of crime. I thought about it for a moment and realized that the only way this would ever *actually* be over is if we killed the Goddess of Fire. She was the obvious mastermind behind all the corruption.

"I think we should go after the Goddess of Fire." I offered strongly. "If we can kill her, we gain the ability to put an end to this finally."

"I agree." Derek said. "We can't sit here and wait for her. She might be stronger, but maybe the surprise aspect will help us."

We both looked at Madisyn.

"Let's get going then."

We exited the colosseum for what I hoped was the last time. We had a singular objective – find the Goddess of Fire and terminate her. Taking Max from us was a terrible mistake she would pay for with her life.

We began our trek back to the library where we last saw her. As it came into our view, we saw that there was barely anything left of it. The whole building burned to the ground and was still roaring with flames.

Either she knew Max was left in the building and torched it, or she thought we were all still in there and no longer her problem. Madisyn and Derek stood back as I searched far and wide.

Fire crackled everywhere as sparks rose into the sky. The smoke began to cloud the air and made it hard to breathe. I almost lost Madisyn and Derek in the smoke. As I made my way back to them, I saw their faces contort with dread.

"Look out!"

I turned around and stiffened as I watched a fireball get closer to my face. Just before it hit me, a loud rumble shook the earth. There was a flash in front of me; a blinding, white light that could only have been *one* person. My blood ran to a chilling halt as I fell to the ground with Frost.

I held his head in my arms to prevent him from smacking it against the concrete. He wore the faintest smile on his face as I cradled him into me.

"Why did you do that?" I scolded him. I felt the coldness of his body begin to vanish slowly. Fire was his weakness.

He lifted his hand up to wipe the tears that were now blurring my vision. The familiar chill I got when he touched me was gone. His power was beginning to fade.

"No, no, please." The tears rushed down my face faster. "Why the hell are you even here? You were supposed to stay in my realm."

"I can actually say I am melting." He attempted to joke. He chuckled weakly and ended it with a cough.

"Even after all this time, you still don't know when to joke." I shook my head at him as I held back a sob. "I can heal you, Frost. Let me heal you,"

"You cannot, Alli." He gulped. "It is too much for you to try to heal."

"Frost, please..."

"I have to say something to you. One...one last thing." He looked at me with his bright, blue eyes beginning to droop. "I am in love with you and I broke the rules. This is to be my fate, forever. Please do not...do not forget what I have taught you...do not forget me."

He was trying so hard to sound stern but I knew he was afraid. He was afraid of the warmth of death. He never had to face it before, after all. His eyes fluttered closed and I screamed while cradling his head into my chest. I shook violently as I gripped the fabric of his shirt in my fingertips.

The loss I felt was staggering and something I never wanted to feel again. I wouldn't wish that feeling on my worst enemy.

His body was cold, but not the frigid temperature I was used to. He didn't have that sharp, bitter iciness to him I slowly grew fond of. He was gone. All that was left was his lifeless body.

All the effort I went through, all the battles and the killing was now for nothing. There would be no happily ever after for Frost and I and I should've known that from the start.

He was gone, and there would be no finding him again.

I grew increasingly angry. The tears of sadness burning my eyes suddenly became tears of fury. The Goddess of Fire just took away the one person I wanted; she took the one person that gave me a reason to live.

"Alli, we have to go." Derek touched my shoulder.

I pushed him off. "Let her find me! Let her try to find me and see if she makes it out alive!" I barked at him.

"Don't be ridiculous, Alliana! She'll kill you!" Madisyn's eyes glimmered with concern as she, too, attempted to stop me.

"And what is there now for me?" I exclaimed, taking both of them aback. "The whole reason I did all of this was for him. He's dead, Madisyn. He's *dead*!" I held Frost's body close to me, not willing to let him go. I couldn't and *wouldn't* leave him behind. He was more than just a person to me.

"He wouldn't want you to do this, Alliana." She whispered while encasing me in her arms. "Be logical about this. You're gonna die too if you just sit here."

"You're right." I rested his head gently against the cement and watched as the ice around him began to melt. "Why wait for her to come for me when I could go get her?"

"Alli, please..."

"I'm going to kill her, Derek." I snapped at him. "I'm going to watch the life fade from her eyes as I have just watched the life fade from Frost's. She will pay for what she has done. All I need is for you guys to stay here with his body. I'll be back." I headed in the direction of the library.

"Alliana, we can't let you go." Madisyn furrowed her eyebrows in worry.

"I'm not asking you to *let* me, Madisyn. Nothing of the sort, actually. I'm going, whether you like it or not."

With that, I turned my back on them and headed towards the burning library. The anger within me was all I needed. I knew I could defeat her. I had absolutely nothing else to lose. First Max, and now Frost. She wanted to take everyone I cared about, so it was time I took her.

That moment the spirit washed away from Frost's eyes would never leave my memory.

The Goddess of Fire would *pay* for what she did.

CHAPTER SIXTEEN

T he pure devastation that I felt was unparalleled. I never really realized how much of my heart he truly was until half of it was completely empty.

After the truly heart-breaking loss of Max, I didn't expect this to happen. Not even in my wildest dreams had I ever pictured losing one of my dearest friends and Frost all in one day.

The whole mission – everything we were trying to do – was for Frost. Without him, there was no physical purpose.

I grieved over the dead body of my lost love as Derek and Madisyn approached the wreckage of the library. They were sent flying backward by an invisible barrier. A shroud of darkness assumed the air around us.

Every power had a different trigger, I learned. Frost's power came so naturally to me that I didn't even realize it. The power of darkness, on the other hand, was so vastly different.

Just like true grief, the darkness consumed everything it touched. The trigger of her power was so simple, yet so...hard to achieve. Pure, relentless misery attacked at the worst moments. All I could do was stay with Frost's memory. Everything I accomplished with him could never be forgotten. His last words were so simple, yet so unforgettable.

Don't forget about me.

I couldn't help but laugh through my tears. Forget him? That would be impossible! The deepest imprint of him on my soul would never allow it. He taught me not only how to use my power to the best of my ability, but how to love unconditionally.

And slowly, that same grief turned into something despicable.

The anger began to rise like a volcano preparing to erupt. She took *everything* from me. It was time to take everything from her.

It was at that moment I knew what I had to do. The Goddess of Fire had caused the last problem she would ever cause again.

As the animosity within me grew stronger, the air became frigid. Ice started to spread across the open clearing. Snow coated the ground within a few short moments. Derek and Madisyn's faces were ridden with fear. They didn't know what I was capable of, and quite frankly, neither did I.

I felt more alive than I ever had. The buildings were glazing over with ice. I was going to find the Goddess of Fire and kill her. Her only chance of survival was killing me first.

I closed my eyes. Once they opened, I saw the fiery trail she left behind. I looked at Derek and Madisyn once again, daring them to follow me. Madisyn put one foot forward, but Derek grabbed her shoulder.

"That's not Alliana anymore." His voice was barely audible over the adrenaline pumping through my veins.

He was right. I wasn't the same person anymore. I was stronger and less dependent on others. I was becoming everything Frost was *supposed* to be – cold and distant with no cares in the world.

Death didn't scare me if it meant I would reunite with Frost once more.

With one single blink, I found myself in front of the building on the other side of the clearing. The very familiar dome of the colosseum drew me in closer to the Goddess of Fire. I couldn't wait to see her emblem go out as I drained every last bit of life from her.

I walked through the halls with a purpose. I approached the double doors without hesitation. I knew she was behind them. I knew she was waiting for me and she was preparing for battle.

I lifted my hand as the doors slammed open in front of me. I walked in to face her. Her back was turned to me as she eyed the portraits of the four remaining trainees. The ice that formed in the clearing was now spread through the room and covered every inch of it.

"I must admit," she turned towards me, "this set of trainees has not made it easy for us."

"You picked the wrong people if easy is what you wanted." I growled at her.

"Oh, dear." she chuckled. "Are you upset about the *pathetic* God of Frost?"

"I'm going to enjoy killing you." Anger flowed through my veins like fire. I stared into her eyes - the same eyes I once believed to be majestic and elegant - and narrowed my own.

"You are not enough." Her voice effortlessly carried throughout the rubble of the destroyed arena. "You're awfully plain and barely skilled in your craft." I swear I felt my blood begin to boil. My skin *burned*.

"You are no better than me."

Her laughter sounded like lava spouting into the chilled ocean. My fists clenched. I could feel the power swirling within me. Only one of us would make it out of this arena - and I had a good idea of who it might be.

"I will never understand what he saw in you."

I froze. She noticed her effect on me.

"He gave...everything...all for you." A sinister grin spread across her face. "He died for nothing." Fury coursed through me.

The grin quickly turned into a frown as a loud rumbling came from deep within the earth.

"He still lives." My nails dug into the skin of my palms as I muttered the words darkly. "He will *always* live within me." She stumbled as the floor began to shake. Derek and Madisyn finally caught up to us. They carefully attempted to push past the ice.

She seemed to notice them shortly after I did. The tips of her fingers began to spark and I knew what she was planning. As soon as the fireball left her palm, I yelled and my own palm opened. One of the columns crumbled. A big chunk of it shot up and collided with her fireball.

The blast sent me shuffling back from my spot, but I stayed

strong on my feet. I saw her, for the first time, afraid of the possible outcome.

"You…" I growled at her. "You…will never take another from me again." The columns began to crumble one by one but she held her ground. I sent one to trap her to the ground, but she quickly shattered it with another fireball.

"You will never defeat me!"

"Oh, but I already have." I gave her the same sickly smile she had once given me as the last column behind her gave way. It landed on top of the Goddess and pinned her to the ground before she even realized what was happening.

"You killed him slowly, you know." I climbed upon the rock that pinned her. "You killed him without remorse…and now he will get his revenge." I felt his presence even though he was gone. A cold chill drifted through the room. It was almost as if he was right next to me, placing his freezing hand upon my shoulder. I breathed in the cold, familiar air and felt more power surge within me.

"He's here…" Her eyes were wide with fear as she struggled beneath the pillar. Her fingers sparked once again, like matches, in a final attempt to stop the advance. I just chuckled and raised my hand quickly. She screamed in pain as a rock fell upon her wrists, holding her down to prevent any use of power.

"He is not the one you should be afraid of." I sneered, looking behind me. Madisyn and Derek watched in horror as I summoned all the water in the realm I could. It began to trickle in a large stream from the doorway until it surrounded the Goddess of Fire. A circle formed around as I kept it from covering her.

It seemed like the one thing she feared the most was the sound of running water.

"Wait!" She called. "Wait, I can help you! You can be the most powerful Goddess in history!"

"I think you're forgetting I've already taken that title." I cackled and allowed the water to inch closer to her. A sizzling sound came from her fingertips as the water lapped at them. She screamed as the water began to take over her arms.

The steam wafted from her as the cold water put her fires out.

"Alliana, the God of Frost would not want you to become a killer!"

"Did he want you to be a killer when you took Max from us?" I snapped. "Enough of this, you're boring me."

The water rose to the top of the pillar I was standing on. Steam rose through the air as bubbles popped at the surface of the water.

In the water, she died slowly. She would feel every ounce of pain Frost felt as the life drained from her. The Goddess of Fire was always a formidable opponent. As I sat there and waited for her end to come, just as I waited for Frost's, I began to wonder one thing: did Max have to die when I had this power in me all along?

I watched until the bubbles stopped floating to the surface. The water slowly drained from the arena and exposed the Goddess in her most vulnerable form. A look of fear remained frozen on her unconscious face.

A beam of intense, red light shot from her seat and the emblem slowly turned to darkness. A sense of relief flooded me as I confirmed she was really gone. All the water left behind was on her drenched body. She would no longer be a danger to me or any of my friends.

A cloud of red drifted from her mouth, just as the dark cloud came from the Goddess of Darkness. This time, I didn't hesitate to take in that power. It shot into me. It felt like smoke clouding my throat as it went down. I grabbed my neck and coughed. I almost fell to my knees before it completely subsided.

Next, a white cloud drifted from her mouth. I was still gasping for air as the smoke feeling dwindled in my throat. I, then, inhaled the white cloud and my body completely dropped in temperature. My hands turned pink, then red, then purple, as I watched my body totally change.

A searing feeling against my wrist caught my attention. The emblem that was burned into my skin was now split into three; darkness, fire, and frost.

I was nauseous. The ground around me seemed to spin as I fell on the pillar I was standing on. I gripped onto the slab of concrete below me trying to find any sense of stability.

None of this would bring Max or Frost back. She took one of my dearest friends and then, shortly after, my dearest love.

I didn't realize Madisyn and Derek were calling my name over and over again until they climbed to the top of the pillar alongside me. Everything around me was a blur as I clambered down with them.

"Alli, it's okay." Madisyn murmured. Her voice echoed in my ears as I attempted to process what she was telling me.

Once I settled in, I realized just how wrong she was. Nothing would ever be okay again. We lost everything important to us and there were still other Gods to handle. I didn't have the strength left to either lose another person or to fight another God.

"Let's get her out of here." Derek told Madisyn.

They practically dragged me down the hallway. I stumbled over my own feet as I tried my best to keep up with them. My throat was dry. Once we made it out of the building, we saw a blizzard raging outside.

I welcomed the snow as comfort. Now, it was just the snow and I. Frost would never be here to finally enjoy his realm with me. He was gone with so much left unsaid. He would never truly know what he meant to me.

We trekked into the tundra, where we were met with Victoria, Apolonia, and the remaining Gods. They stood in a broad circle that Madisyn, Derek, and I completed.

The Goddess of Wind, the God of Earth, and the God of Healing were standing uniformly with their hands behind their backs.

"What's going on?" Derek whispered as he exchanged a glance with Madisyn.

"You've got me." Madisyn shook her head.

The God of Earth stepped forward and bowed his head to me. "Alliana, we always knew you were meant for great things." The blizzard still raged around us.

"What are you talking about?" I asked even though my head was still fuzzy.

"Through the loss of Maximo and the God of Frost, you have completed a task no one has been able to before." The God of Healing stepped forward next.

"The Goddess of Fire has been our leader for millennia. By killing her, you have taken her place." The Goddess of Wind continued.

Then, all three of them, together, finished their speech.

"We welcome you as our leader and bow to you always."

CHAPTER SEVENTEEN

For what felt like weeks, I moped around the halls the Gods begun rebuilding. The realm was coming back together nicely. Although Frost's realm belonged to me now, I didn't feel comfortable coming and going as I pleased. I chose not to go back since the initial visit.

There were many times the Gods, new and old, asked me for advice. There was nothing I could say to them because I was barely mentally capable of taking care of myself. The loss of both Frost and Max was still weighing heavily on me.

The place had become...dry and almost *boring* without Max. Madisyn came to visit me often, but she was the only person I saw. Derek assumed his position as the God of Fire. Apolonia was the new Goddess of Light.

Madisyn acquired the power of water due to both God and trainee being eliminated in the war. Despite having the power of darkness myself, I granted Victoria the power as well. I held tightly onto the power of frost.

I was the leader of the Gods but felt so small and irrelevant. I decided, after a couple of weeks of moping, I would leave them to their devices. I packed what little I had in this realm in one bag.

I didn't tell anyone I was leaving or where I was going. I appeared in front of the familiar door to my mother's house. I held back tears as I knocked on the door. My mother opened it. She saw the look on my face and ushered me in quickly.

There was something so special about the bond I had with my mother. I didn't have to tell her what was wrong, but she probably figured the lack of Frost's presence wasn't a good thing. For the first time in weeks, I allowed myself to break down.

In my realm, I wasn't the leader of the Gods nor was I a murderer. In my realm, I was my mother's child who sometimes liked to leave home intermittently with no explanation. Here, I wasn't the strongest being in the land. I was a girl just slowly becoming an adult. Nobody knew the kinds of terrors I went through shortly before coming home.

I lived at such a *normal* pace for a few weeks that I began to miss using my power. I always heeded the warning Frost gave me when I was younger. The townsfolk here knew nothing of magic and would feel threatened by its presence.

There was something so...unsatisfying with staying at home. This small town led people nowhere. Nobody here was *destined* for greatness. Nobody left. Everyone stayed in this tiny village from the day of their birth until the day of their death.

These things weighing on my mind really made me appreciate how much I actually fit into the world of the Gods. As if giving me a sign, or something to help me make my decision, there was a knock at the front door.

When I opened it, I was greeted by Madisyn and Derek. I almost started crying at the sight of the people who fought alongside me. Madisyn was dressed in the prettiest ocean blue color I'd ever seen and Derek in the bright red color his mentor always used to wear. They smiled as they saw me.

"Alli, it's been a while." Derek's smile was wide.

"Yeah." I nodded and looked down at my plain clothes. "What do you need?"

"You need to come back." Madisyn whispered. "It's unrest there. We need a leader. The Goddess of Wind thinks she's in charge now that you're not there."

"As if," I scoffed and rolled my eyes, "that girl couldn't even properly formulate a tornado to kill us."

"We need you, Alli." Derek added. "With the realm rebuilt, the old Gods want to take on trainees again and prepare for another war."

I froze. The shock on my face was evident as I met Derek's eyes.

"Another war?" I furrowed my eyebrows. "Are they insane?"

"Well, they're used to doing it over and over again. They aren't sure how that's going to work under new leadership." Madisyn told me. "They're so used to their old ways they don't even see an issue with it."

"We can't risk losing anyone else." I shook my head quickly. "I'm sorry, but I can't go back."

"Frost's realm has been unoccupied for too long." Madisyn continued. "Alliana, all of the things in it will slowly begin to fade away unless it is occupied. It's too cold for us, but we've tried to at least go for a little bit."

"It's *hard*, Madisyn..."

"Are you serious right now?" She scoffed with a short laugh escaping her lips. "You think it's been hard for *you*? We lost them too, you know. We lost a *lot* of people in the war. But news flash, nobody ran away except for *you*. You knew what you were taking on when you killed the Goddess of Fire. So, stop being the weak Goddess she expected you to be and start being what *Frost* knew you to be."

Derek grabbed her arm but she jerked it away.

"We can't force her to go, Madisyn." Derek told her.

"Frost knew you would be a Goddess of unspeakable power. That's why he was willing to die for you. If you really want to make his death for nothing, then fine. Stay here. But we'll be waiting for you back where you belong."

Derek disappeared in a cloud of smoke and Madisyn turned into a puddle on the ground. I sighed and leaned against my door frame.

At the end of the day, she was right. Frost wanted me to be the strongest I could possibly be. Shortly after they left, I made my decision.

I was going to go back and put an end to their ridiculous ideas of starting another war. We would never put innocent people through that again. Nobody else would ever have to suffer the losses I did.

I delved deep into the closet in my bedroom. In the very back was an outfit I took from the realm of the Gods - the pure white jumpsuit that had the frost emblem stitched into the sleeve.

Finally, I put myself together and I pulled the outfit on. I walked into my bathroom, for what I knew was the last time, and I made myself look neat. My hair grew down to the middle of my back. I tied it into a tight, high ponytail.

As I took one last glance at my house, I willed myself into the other realm. The realm looked just as it did the first time I saw it. Everything was put back together and flourishing. The buildings stood taller than they did the last time they were built. There was a new building in the center. It stood colossal and proud as it taunted me to walk inside.

The doors opened as I neared them. Walking into this building was something so foreign. The torches were replaced with large chandeliers and the floors were made of a gold-looking marble. The walls were white with flecks of gold in them to match the floor. It sparkled in the light of the chandelier.

At the end of the hallway was a set of double doors. Those swung open as I lifted my hand. The seven other Gods and Goddesses ceased their yelling and arguing. They saw my presence in the room and stood straight up.

There was a gleam of hope in Madisyn's eyes as I met her glance. I nodded slightly at her. Her harsh and true words were the turning point to make me opt for my decision. They all sat at a round table. The biggest, most extravagant chair was empty. My emblem shone brightly at the top center of it.

"Take your seats." I said coldly. I watched as they all sat in unison. "I am not quite sure where you all got the idea that there would be *another* war, but you were misled. Nothing of the sort will be allowed under my leadership." I walked around the table until I found my seat. There was something so...tempting about sitting in that very chair.

"As the newly acclaimed Goddess of Frost, you may not know

how things have always operated around here." The Goddess
of Wind interjected. "We have always done this. We obtain our
trainees and train them to the best of our ability, and then we
fight them with intent to kill."

"Did you not hear one word that I said?" I snapped at her. "You
are under new leadership. The Goddess of Fire was the one who
made you fight your trainees. She made the rules that led to the
demise of the God of Frost, my predecessor."

"All due respect, Goddess of Frost, but I think you are the one
that is mistaken." The God of Earth cleared his throat. "We have
already begun the selection process of the next trainees."

"The only way we take on trainees is if they are truthfully
going to take over for us." I corrected him. "Unless you are willing
to step down when the trainee is ready to assume your position,
you are not to select a trainee."

"The War made all of us prove ourselves worthy of the
position, Goddess of Frost." Victoria, the new Goddess of
Darkness, stated. "How are we to know our new trainees are
worthy of our spot if they do not fight for it?"

"Your selection process better be foolproof." I told her sternly.
I turned to look at the other Gods that remained from the last
group. "If you three begin to think you can do something like
that under my nose, I will have no issues killing you and finding
someone to replace you. Do not say I never warned you."

Everyone's eyes were on me, waiting for the next words I was
formulating.

"As for your challenges for said trainees...make new ones.
Do not use the ones of your predecessors. This meeting is
adjourned."

The Gods and Goddesses all stood and quickly shuffled out
the set of double doors. This room was similar to the colosseum I
once did my challenges in. I looked to my left to see the portraits
lining the walls.

The seven portraits hung prominently. The God of Earth
and the Goddess of Wind had the same portrait they did when I
started my challenges. Seeing the strong faces of Madisyn, Derek,

Apolonia, and Victoria as portraits was something surreal. I couldn't help but realize how much better it would be if Frost and Max remained up there as well. Even my portrait in the middle seemed off.

The end of the war was certainly not the end of our problems. There was a clear rift between the old Gods and the new. There were ways of the old that needed to end with the ways of the new.

The cycle would keep going. There would always be someone more powerful than the first. I hoped by ending the war, my psychological trauma would eventually fade too. There was always going to be this empty hole in my heart where Frost used to reside.

I thought of what Madisyn told me, about how Frost's realm was slowly disappearing. I remembered how cold it was the first time I was in it, and I couldn't help but wonder *why*. As I entered his realm again for the first time since that night, it oddly felt like *home*.

The residual effects of him there were evident. When I opened my eyes, a blizzard was raging in front of me in a vast, open field. The snow was piling higher and higher by the second. This realm screamed everything Frost had taught me. I belonged here in the cold, watching snowflakes melt against my skin.

In front of me, seemingly waiting for me, was Gelum, Frost's beloved wolf. He tilted his head at me as if he expected Frost to be there as well. Gelum lived for centuries with only Frost. I wasn't sure how he would handle the loss.

I squatted down. The cold welcomed me as Gelum trotted over with his tail in between his legs. I pet his surprisingly dry fur. His familiar, bright, blue eyes stared directly into mine. I knew he felt the loss of Frost just as I had.

The tears gathered in my eyes as he nuzzled into my shoulder. A short whine of despair escaped his mouth.

"It'll be okay, boy." I gave him a sad smile. "I miss him too."

EPILOGUE

Decades had gone by. Our realm since became shrouded with peace. There were no issues between the Gods and there were no wars planned. The God of Earth recently decided it was time for him to resign, so he brought in a new trainee to take his place a few years back.

I loved the peace I brought upon the realm. After careful decision making, I realized it was time for me to step down as well. Leadership was not something people could perfect overnight, but I didn't see myself as the best leader.

I chose a trainee almost five years ago. My trainee was very accustomed because he possessed an extraordinary amount of power as soon as he was born into the world. Madisyn and Derek both begged me not to give up my position.

We entered this battle together all those years ago. They didn't want to lose anyone else just yet. Of course, I would still have to teach my trainee. I would have to show him how to use his power and how to master it. He would take a lot of work, just as I took a lot of work for Frost.

The first time I physically met my trainee would be on his tenth birthday. He was similar to me when I was younger. He would always spend time in his favorite, hidden-away spot.

His hideaway spot wasn't flowers and a vast, empty field. He enjoyed exploring caves and hidden areas that nobody otherwise would find. He was a very special boy. He found his way out of even the most difficult of situations.

I realized, as I watched the child grow, this was exactly what Frost did with me. The reason he felt so connected with me was because he watched over me my whole life. Time and time again, he anonymously helped me make my decisions.

I knew deep inside my heart this was something I had to do. This was not an opportunity I could pass up – not with so much on the line.

The War was a distant memory. Nobody even saw the benefits of it anymore. The Gods and Goddesses alike were all in agreeance for once. The Goddess of Wind was my biggest contender. I tried multiple times to convince her to step down, but she wouldn't have it. She was determined to be the next leader of the Gods.

However, she was going to be severely disappointed when she found out I planned on naming my trainee the new leader. She held a grudge with Frost and she held one with me just the same.

With all of this time behind me, there was no longer a purpose for me to be the leader. I would give up my title and then live out the rest of my time in Frost's realm. The snow became a comfort for me, as well as Gelum.

I watched from afar as the child ran towards the newest cave he found. He enjoyed climbing and risking his life in unknown places. He was so familiar, yet so different.

I made myself visible to him. The ground froze beneath my feet as it did for Frost when I first met him.

The kid turned to me with a familiar pair of dazzling, blue eyes meeting mine. His hair was dark and messy. He tilted his head as he looked at me. He wasn't *scared*. Nothing scared this child.

I couldn't help but smile at him as I recognized what was happening. Just as Frost watched over me, I did the same for the boy.

Welcome back, Frost. I thought to myself before repeating the same line that was said to me when we first met.

"Do not fear, young one." My voice carried with the wind. "I am not here to hurt you."

ABOUT THE AUTHOR

Haley Warrington is a nineteen-year-old who has been writing her whole life. She has always enjoyed creative writing and always dreamed of writing a novel. The idea of being published was always so far-fetched to her, and now she is living her dream! Through a lot of dedication, hard work, and late nights, she has finally finished her first of many books.

CPSIA information can be obtained
at www.ICGtesting.com
Printed in the USA
BVHW041645080221
599347BV00010B/84